The Forty First Wink

JAMES WALLEY

RAGNAROK PUBLICATIONS
CRESTVIEW HILLS, KENTUCKY

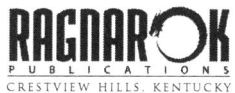

THE FORTY FIRST WINK
Ragnarok Publications | www.ragnarokpub.com
Editor In Chief: Tim Marquitz | Creative Director: J.M. Martin
The Forty First Wink is copyright © 2014 by James Walley.
All rights reserved.

The characters and events portrayed in this book are fictitious or fictitious recreations of actual historical persons. Any similarity to real persons, living or dead, is coincidental and not intended by the authors unless otherwise specified. This book or any portion thereof may not be reproduced or used in any manner whatsoever without the express written permission of the publisher except for the use of brief quotations in a book review.

Published by Ragnarok Publications
206 College Park Drive, Ste. 1
Crestview Hills, KY 41017

ISBN-13: 978-0-9903909-1-6
Worldwide Rights
Created in the United States of America

Publicity: Melanie R. Meadors
Social Media: Nick Sharps
Cover Design & Interior Layout: Shawn T. King

Dedicated to my parents, who provided me with the tools to write this story. Without your unwavering support, it would still be a random collection of crazy ideas bouncing around in my head.

There are of course, many more people who have found their way onto my Christmas card list thanks to their input and assistance, most notably, the following amazing human beings. My family for being animated and affirming at every turn, I wish I could mention you all by name. Danny Kouble for providing fantastic cover art on the original version of this book. My own unofficial advertisers, Emma Lea, Katie Lajoie and David Eccles for raising profile and spreading the word. My good friends Mark O'Neill, Paul Carson and Paula Kasser for indispensable advice and drunken brainstorming.

Huge appreciation must also go out to Tim Marquitz, Joe Martin, Shawn King, and the rest of the awesome folks at Ragnarok for providing me with this opportunity. A special mention to the authors therein for welcoming me so warmly into the fold.

This doesn't begin to cover the number of people who have provided inspiration and motivation, both directly and indirectly. Rest assured though, that I am immensely thankful to all who had a hand in this story's creation, particularly to the people who may see something of themselves in a character or two.

Morning

Not well versed in the proper protocol of rising with enthusiasm and vigor, morning came with the same ache and confusion as a zombie awakening with that insatiable craving to snack on some brains. A night in the company of tequila was no doubt in some way responsible.

It was with this lingering, half-remembered recollection of the night before that Marty was reintroduced to the break of day. Eyelids heavy like storm shutters, pulling back to reveal the sun's gleeful intrusion into his room.

The monkey sitting on his chest started at his stirring, nearly dropping the polo mallet he had, up until now, been using to beat out a tune on Marty's forehead. Polo monkey blinked, seemingly alarmed and upset at the interruption of his drum solo. His monkey cohorts, sensing they had been rumbled, deserted their posts and scattered, one dropping the keys he had been stowing in a sock, another caught in the act of swallowing a handful of pocket change.

Through his tequila-inspired malaise, Marty wondered why his fleeing bedfellows were all wearing little blue uniforms with matching hats, which sported the kind of strobing lights you might normally see atop angry police cars. Through such a haze, though, and because his tiny tormentors had vacated with such haste, this thought registered merely as a muffled array of noise and movement, coupled with the sort of confusion only obtained from being abruptly awoken by a bunch of monkeys in your bedroom.

Marty rolled over and tried to ignore the dull throbbing in his head that had been polo-malletted into sharp clarity in the last few minutes. This was normally the point where one vowed to never drink again, and actually mean it, even though it was lots of fun and would probably seem like a great idea again in the not too distant future.

"They'll be back you know."

The voice was high pitched but carried a faint growl, as though its owner had ingested a combination of helium and gravel. It came from the corner of the room where the shadows cast by the morning sun barely obscured a slightly ajar cupboard door.

"They normally don't stop until you throw up, or at least go and find something fried to eat."

Marty made an attempt at focusing on a vague stab at coherence. It was still a good way off. Nevertheless, having a conversation with a squeaky-voiced cupboard didn't seem to be out of place this morning, and he was already wondering what all this was about.

Marty engaged his brain, and it grudgingly obliged. "What? Who, the…the little monkey fellas? The beer monkeys?"

He tasted alcohol and smacked his lips disapprovingly, rubbing his eyes and groaning.

"I've had many visits from the beer monkeys. They've never stuck around until I've woken up before, though," Marty imparted through gritted teeth.

The voice gravel-squeaked again. "They prefer the term *hangover technicians*, and you interrupted them. You'll probably get a letter now."

"A letter? They're monkeys," Marty managed.

"They have a quota," the cupboard squeaker replied. "Put enough monkeys in a room with a typewriter and they'll write Shakespeare. Imagine what they can do when they're unionized."

As fascinating as this conversation was becoming, the seed of delicious fried breakfast delights had been sown in Marty's mind, and although his stomach was staging a fairly steadfast protest of the whole concept, some form of morning after fry up was inevitable. This would, however, involve a degree of movement, a maneuver that Marty's brain was still attempting to orchestrate.

With a groan, limbs were called into action, and Marty shifted into a vaguely upright position. Phase one of Operation Damage Control was now officially underway.

His stomach dialed up its protests to Def Con 4.

As everyone knows, the hangover fry up is an essential part of casting out the demons of the previous night's merriment, but as Marty's bladder interjected, a more pressing matter would need to be attended to first.

Shakily, and with all the grace of a baby gazelle ice skating through a mine field, Marty lurched towards the bathroom. Reaching the door was a victory, and before he knew what he was doing, Marty had pulled the light cord turning on what felt like a nuclear blast behind his eyes.

Reeling, he heard the cupboard offer up some squeaky advice, "Don't bother with the lights. Just fire when ready."

Sound advice, quickly taken with a hasty tug of the light cord.

Stumbling around in the bathroom, now thankfully returned to its darkened state, Marty located the toilet and took his best shot. Under the circumstances, hitting anything porcelain would have been a bonus, so hearing the reassuring sound of the bowl being christened was a relief. Soon he was shambling out of the door and trying to remember which way the kitchen was.

"You didn't wash your hands," came a shrill protest from the cupboard.

"Ahh, shut up, cupboard, I need bacon," Marty shot back over his shoulder as he vacated the bedroom.

The voice from the cupboard muttered at the empty room as the bedroom door signified Marty's departure.

"The name's Timbers."

In the hallway on the other side of the bedroom door was a large, three quarter length mirror. Marty always used it as a final inspection point when on his way out to make sure everything was where it should be and nothing had been missed in the grooming and dressing process. Flies unzipped, hair out of place, or something unpleasant dangling out of his nose, for example. It wasn't really for, and shouldn't really have been used for hangover damage assessment, and yet Marty stopped in front of it to take stock of the current situation.

He stared blearily at his reflection and decided that the whole never drinking again idea had come a day too late. Still, the damage was superficial and could easily be fixed by a fry up and a couple of aspirin.

Marty understood the hangover ritual well, having gone through the drill more than a few times. Now a good way into his twenties, he spent the beginnings of his weekends like most people his age did, and the latter parts regretting it, like most people his age do.

Having successfully navigated life to this point, though, Marty had hit a bit of a speed bump and was, it seemed, replaying the same weekend over and over again. It was easy to do since he was very good at the drinking part and had become quite adept at handling what inevitably came afterwards. Not a professional, of course, since he didn't go to meetings or stand outside pubs waiting for them to open. More an enthusiast of indulgence.

The fact that his life hadn't really panned out how he'd thought when he left university didn't really seem that important. He had a roof over his head, which he rented from a nice Indian gentleman who ran a shop in the town. He had money coming in, although he wouldn't have classed what he did as a job or career, as this would suggest some form of future. And aside from a promotion to the donut kiosk, cavorting around in a Harvey the Space Beagle costume at the local theme park didn't really offer much in the way of prospects.

Originally, Marty had harbored dreams of becoming an artist, but as with most dreams, unless they are backed by commitment and drive they just don't pay the bills, and so he had taken the job to supplement his income. He'd just never gotten around to actually getting on with the dream part. Still, he was only twenty-something, that time of your life when you are supposed to make bad judgment calls and generally bum around for a bit, surely.

Marty's eyes met his unshaven reflection. Things would be all right; they were bound to be. The bloodshot, unkempt look would be dealt with, and he'd be ready to take on the world again, or at least whatever the world wanted to throw his way.

He pointed at the mirror, smiled and made a clicking sound. "Don't go anywhere. I'll be right back," he said in an over the top Southern drawl before heading off down the hall towards the kitchen.

His reflection in the mirror watched him leave. As

the kitchen door opened, and then shut behind Marty, mirror Marty smiled, rolled his eyes, and shook his head.

The kitchen was small and functional and seemed infinitely more awake than the rest of the flat, its curtainless window allowing the morning sun to stream in unfettered. Marty's eyes adjusted to the intruding daylight, and he quickly made for the fridge. Fishing out the relevant breakfast components, he realized he would have to do what every kitchen procrastinator dreads: a bit of washing up.

The sink was not a warzone, but it was partially obscured by a few dishes and a pan that had been left to soak. No problem when the reward of breakfast was in the offing. Soon, several strips of bacon and a couple of eggs were sizzling away on the cooker.

Marty drew himself a glass of water and swallowed some aspirin. The day was already starting to look better, and the smell of the bacon was delivering some weighty body blows to his retreating hangover. Waiting for breakfast to cook, Marty started to whistle, and though almost completely awake, he did not notice that several birds, perched on the bird table outside the window, were whistling along in unison.

If this had caught his attention, he may even have noticed they had also formed what appeared to be a conga line and were dancing up and down the table merrily. He did not, however, and the impromptu song and dance routine went unnoticed, which was rather a shame because they were making quite a good fist of it.

His breakfast ready, Marty quickly sat down and dove in. Between mouthfuls he tried to recall the events of the night before. There had been tequila, that had already been established, and some kind of celebration involving a birthday, but other than that there were still gaping holes in his memory. At least he had woken up at home and undamaged, which was a big plus.

Only then, as his breakfast and painkillers set about reducing his hangover to tolerable levels, did he remember the manner of his awakening. There had been monkeys. Monkeys and a talking cupboard. This was much harder to rationalize, and Marty's brow furrowed. He finished off the last of the bacon and rubbed his temples, his mind now fully committed to deciphering whether that had actually happened, or whether he was in fact still a little drunk. Or insane. Or both.

Whatever the explanation, he decided he would have to investigate further. Not being a cat, he figured a bit of curiosity would do no harm at all and headed with purpose back into the hallway, passing the birds in the window, who were now engaged in a spirited can-can dance, which again, alas, went completely unnoticed.

Marching up the hallway, Marty passed the mirror and glanced at his reflection,

"Morning!" Mirror Marty chimed

"Yeah, good morning," Marty replied absently. He was on a mission and had no time to exchange pleasantries with himself.

Opening the door, he found the bedroom to be less gloomy than it had been when he left it, although that could have been the hangover. Shards of sunlight pried their way in through the gaps in the curtains and fell in crisscrossed patterns across the floor.

It wasn't particularly messy, but the array of clothes discarded from last night still lay beside the bed and a small stack of CDs had been knocked over. Tom Jones smiled up at Marty cheekily from within a plastic case.

The adjoining bathroom door was still ajar from his recent visit and a clothes hamper stood overflowing in the corner next to it. On the far wall was a desk littered with sketches, doodles, and various art paraphernalia. A spotlight leaned in, and dangling from it was a key ring with a picture of Harvey the Space Beagle grinning cheerily from within an oversized space helmet.

Next to that, the cupboard. Its slatted door open, but seemingly not quite as talkative as it had been earlier. This was Marty's wardrobe, and although he also kept shoes, books, and various other knickknacks in there, he could not remember ever storing anything in there that had a squeaky-gravelly voice.

"Erm…hello…?"

The quiet of the room was broken, and Marty felt a little foolish as he made his enquiry to the cupboard.

"Is anyone in there?"

For a moment, silence was restored in the room, and Marty started to think maybe he had overdone it slightly last night. Then the cupboard replied.

"Hello! Are you feeling better?"

It was the same squeak-gravel voice as before, and Marty jumped back, startled.

"Umm, I'm not sure," he managed. "I think I might be going mad. I'm talking to a cupboard."

The voice chuckled. "Or talking to what's in the cupboard?"

"No, I don't think so. None of my shoes talk."

Marty edged closer, picking up a slipper and brandishing it over his head. Cautiously, he pushed the cupboard door fully open and peered inside. Shirts and coats hung from a rail and a shoe tree dangled from a hook in the corner, filled with non-talking shoes. An open box filled with books and magazines sat in the corner next to a set of bongo drums and a traffic cone. Marty squinted and cleared his throat.

"Who's in here?"

"Down here," the voice chirped again from behind the box of books.

Marty shifted his gaze to the box. There was nothing there. Just books, the drums, the traffic cone, and a small doll dressed as a pirate.

The pirate doll nodded at Marty and waved. "Avast!" it squealed happily.

Marty leapt several feet backwards, letting out an involuntary yelp and tripping over the partner of the slipper he held in his hand. Scrambling to his feet, he thrust his makeshift club out in front of him as the little pirate doll trotted out of the cupboard and stood proudly, hands on hips, spot lit by a shaft of morning sunlight.

"I thought you'd be happier to see me. What are you planning on doing with that?" enquired the tiny buccaneer, pointing at Marty's slipper.

There are many things that would doubtless go through a person's mind when faced with a talking toy. What Marty managed, although not particularly incisive, was probably the most pertinent thing to say given the circumstances.

"Who? What?"

The little pirate looked quizzically at Marty. "Well, the 'what' part seems to involve you having some sort of fit, and as for 'who', I thought you would have recognized old Timbers!"

"Timbers? But I haven't seen you since I was five!" Marty's head spun. He was certain that his mother had given Timbers away years ago with the rest of his childhood toys. He was also certain that Timbers hadn't been this talkative when he was a child. He was, however, exactly how Marty remembered him, minus the whole talking thing.

Standing about two feet tall, the little sack cloth pirate had a broad grin stitched onto his face, which displayed more gaps than teeth. One black beady eye was accompanied by a leather eye patch covering the other. An impressive looking scar had been sewn onto his right cheek, and his chin was a mass of stubbly wool. He wore an oversized tri-cornered hat perched rakishly atop his head, which carried the trademark skull and bones logo, although it was cartoon like and friendly looking. In keeping with the look, he also sported a felt blue frock coat with shiny gold trim and huge gold buttons, a frilled white felt shirt beneath and faded brown felt trousers. The ensemble was completed by a pair of black leather cavalier boots with gleaming silver buckles. From his belt hung a cutlass with an ornately curved gold hilt, and on his other hip, a tiny plastic flintlock pistol.

Now the grin vanished and was replaced by a pursed-lipped look of uncertainty. Timbers' brow was furrowed and he was scratching his wool stubble thoughtfully. "What's the matter? You look like you've seen a ghost."

"No, I think a ghost would be slightly less worrying," blurted Marty, who had backed away and come to rest in his desk chair, slipper still held out tamely in an attempt to look threatening. "I'm not even at work yet and already inanimate objects are talking to me." At the theme park it was cute and mildly amusing, here though, seeing a toy pirate advancing out of his bedroom cupboard and saying hello was definitely several miles the wrong side of strange.

Timbers had ceased his advance and was standing, hands on hips again, head to one side, as he regarded Marty curiously. "Work? You don't 'work' here. As far as I'm aware, nobody actually works here. Why would anyone dream about working? That's just twisted…well, unless your work involves ale or pies or nudity or something."

Marty's fevered, panicked expression dissolved instantly as he grasped what Timbers had just said. "A dream? I'm dreaming? Of course, obviously this isn't happening. I'm not here talking to Blackbeard's action figure, I'm asleep. I'm dreaming!" He was almost giggling with relief. The thought he might, in actual fact, be going a bit peculiar had started to take root when this odd conversation had started, but logic was now making an appearance, albeit a fleeting one as Timbers interjected.

"Dreaming? No, you're not dreaming. Well, not really. I mean, you're a dream aren't you?"

Marty let out a short, uncomfortable sounding chuckle. A few awkward moments passed before he finally cleared his throat and darted a glance sheepishly at Timbers. "Well I'm flattered you think so, but in all honesty I'm not sure how to react to a compliment from a talking toy."

Timbers held his hands up and took a few steps towards Marty, "No, no, no, I don't mean…wait, something's not right here."

Marty, now confused beyond words, managed some anyway. "The word understatement doesn't quite do that statement justice." He stared off into the corner of the room, nervously chewing his lip and absently twirling a pencil between his fingers, clearly attempting to funnel in the vast amount of new information the morning had delivered.

Timbers, who had busied himself with shimmying up the

table leg during this lull in proceedings, strode purposefully across the table and appeared at Marty's shoulder.

"Look, I know it sounds..." he began. The conclusion of that sentence was lost however, as Marty suddenly snapped back from his trance, whirled in shock and caught Timbers in the chest with the slipper he was still clutching.

The little pirate pinwheeled backwards and loosed a tiny, shrill "Arrrrrr!" that would have sounded hilarious in other circumstances, and vanished head first over the side of the desk.

Now completely overbalanced on the chair, Marty spun wildly, legs inexplicably both in the air at once, hands grasping at nothing as he tried in vain to make a graceful transition from the seated position to the sprawled on the floor position. With a resounding *thud*, he completed this maneuver with a glancing blow on the side of the table, which sent paper and pencils skittering in all directions and sent Marty spectacularly crashing to a painful rest on the floor.

The moment it took to register what had just happened after falling duly passed, and Marty struggled to his feet, wincing at a sharp jolt of pain that was now dancing up and down his arm. He scanned the floor. Timbers lay face down, motionless, and bent impossibly back on himself against a waste paper bin at the foot of the desk.

Hesitantly, Marty limped towards the stricken pirate, now seemingly as lifeless as a toy ought to be. Reaching down, he nudged Timbers' foot. Nothing. Again he nudged the tiny leather boot, and still there was no response. Grabbing the boot, Marty twisted and lifted, and Timbers flopped over onto his back, his one good eye staring blankly at the ceiling.

Silent moments passed and Marty wondered with increasing concern whether, having been undoubtedly the first person in the world to converse with a living stuffed toy, he was also now the first person in the world to have killed a stuffed toy. Briefly, he considered how one would go about delivering CPR to a two foot tall pirate doll, but then wondered how he would check for a pulse, or even whether Timbers was actually breathing. These questions danced around Marty's head briefly like absurd, sanity-threatening pixies before he finally decided it was time to act.

Squatting down in front of the tiny prostrate figure, he again cleared his throat in an 'Excuse me, hello?' sort of way.

"Erm…Timbers…Timbers, are you…" Marty raised an eyebrow and shrugged, "…alive?"

Timbers sat bolt upright, coughing dryly. "Ya scurvy dog! That was a cheap shot."

Marty sprang backwards, arms outstretched apologetically. "I'm sorry, I'm sorry, you startled me. Are you all right?"

"You broadsided me! If I had a plank handy, you'd be walking it now, me hearty." Timbers, already up on his feet, had drawn his cutlass and was waving it threateningly to and fro. Unfortunately, however, his hat had slid down over his good eye, and the cuts, thrusts, and lunges being directed at Marty were instead being aimed at the now overturned desk chair.

"Please, calm down, it was an accident," Marty implored, but Timbers' swash was fully buckled, and he continued with his squeaky ranting.

Although the little pirate was now whirling like a top, Marty managed to grab a handful of collar and hoist Timbers into the air, provoking a startled squeak, which punctuated his now barely audible grumbling and cursing.

"Please, just stop for a second. I don't want a fight…stop!"

Timbers ceased his struggling and raised a hand to adjust his hat. Finally able to see, he squinted up at Marty and grimaced.

"All right, you got me. Nice move with the slipper."

"Look, I'm sorry. I didn't mean to hit you. Are you hurt?"

Timbers seemed to be cheered by the apology, and the partially toothed smile returned. "Hurt? Well, of course not. We can't get hurt. Well, not really. I mean yeah it hurt, but I'm not…hurt. You see what I mean?"

Marty really didn't.

He let go of his handful of collar and Timbers dropped to the ground, where he deftly sheathed his cutlass and set about adjusting his manhandled coat. Looking at Marty, he gave a friendly nod and pumped his fists in a playful, pugilistic gesture.

"Looks like I got off a few shots, too. You look knackered."

The little stitched smile receded again, and a little sack

cloth finger pointed at the patchy bruise that was making its way across Marty's shoulder. "Hang on, that's not right. You look hurt. I mean hurt-hurt, not…"

"Can we not go into that again please?" Marty interrupted, as he, too, became aware of the source of the pain he had experienced in his recent tumble. "I need some ice for this."

Holding his shoulder gingerly, he headed for the bedroom door, glancing back over his shoulder as he did so. "Don't go anywhere, erm, Timbers. I'll be back in a minute, and then I want some answers."

"You and me both, matey!" The miniature corsair shouted after Marty.

Marty closed the bedroom door behind him and leaned against it, wincing as he did so. Some ice, or a bag of peas or something similar was needed from the freezer, but more importantly, what the hell was going on?

Unsurprisingly, a conversation and subsequent scuffle with a half-remembered toy from his childhood had not thrown up too many answers, but it had proven beyond any doubt that something was definitely amiss.

Hmm, yes, about four hundred or so miles amiss, give or take.

That would have to wait, though. Pain has a way of becoming a priority, and even though the aspirin he'd chased down with breakfast were dealing mortal blows to his hangover, the post pirate fight injuries would need to be dealt with separately.

Marty shifted from against the door and made for the kitchen, passing the mirror in the hallway again as he did so.

"Ouch! Someone's caught you a right doozy there, haven't they?"

The voice behind him was familiar, and Marty stopped dead, wondering whether to turn and discover who had spoken, or given the preceding events of the morning so far, to just make a run for it.

Was discretion the better part of valor? He couldn't remember. What happened to he who fought and ran away? Did he laugh longest? How many was a bird in the hand worth? His mind had gone totally blank.

His eyes tightly shut, Marty turned.

The complete absence of anything horrendous, life-threatening, or even noteworthy caused curiosity to once again get the better of him, and Marty opened one eye, and then the other, to be greeted by the sight of absolutely nothing.

The hallway was deserted, and only his reflection stared back at him from the three-quarter-length mirror on the wall.

Instinctively, Marty reached up and put a hand to his face. He wasn't smiling. So why was his reflection peering back at him with a smug, knowing grin?

"My, we are a handsome chap aren't we?" The voice rang out again, and this time, Marty could see it was coming from the face in the mirror. *His* face.

"Are you just going to stand there? It's a bit rude not to acknowledge a compliment, even if it is from yourself."

Marty blinked, then rubbed his eyes, then moved closer to the mirror, studying his own image as it copied his movements in absolutely no way whatsoever. His face almost touching the mirror, Marty waved a hand in the hope of seeing his reflection do the same thing. It didn't. The same smug expression remained fixed on its face.

At last, Marty found some words. "I'm sorry, is this some kind of trick?" He touched the mirror cautiously. "Can today get any more weird?"

"I suspect it just might."

Mirror Marty's reply shocked his real counterpart back a few steps, but he had spoken, and of his own volition. The voice was definitely Marty's, although it had a faint echo and a strange, unnatural quality to it, as though it had been spoken backwards, and then played back in reverse.

"This might seem like a stupid question," Marty ventured, "but, who are you?"

His image in the mirror chuckled, "Well, I'm you, obviously. I bet this is really taking your head for a spin isn't it?"

In a morning of understatements, this one was a genuine contender for the gold medal spot, and while Marty's brain struggled to get a handle on the situation, his legs decided it might be a good time to take a time out. He slumped into a vaguely seated position against the wall opposite his reflection. "Please," he mustered. "What the hell is going on?"

"Oh, you want answers? Well, you're in luck, my friend, I have answers, but you already know what they are. You see, I am your Id."

Mirror Marty folded his arms and beamed as though he had just imparted the secret of the universe. However, since this revelation only drew a blank expression from Marty, his likeness continued. "This is going to take a bit of explaining isn't it?"

Marty nodded distantly, his brow still contorted in a frozen display of disbelief and confusion.

"Right, ok then. To put it as plainly as I can, you appear to have woken up in your own dream. I know this because I have been here many times. It really is great fun, I get to do whatever I want to because it's my dream to shape and cultivate how I please. You see, your Id is the part of you that contains your basic drives and instincts. It compels you to eat that fourth doughnut and down that last drink you really shouldn't have. So as you can imagine, it's pretty much anything goes here for me.

"Honestly, I can do anything I like here. There was this one time I was driving an open-topped busload of nuns through a car wash…" Mirror Marty's smile broadened and his eyes glazed for a moment, "…but I digress. The point is, my fun is always short lived. You wake up in your bed, and I have to climb back into the little box in your head. That is, until this morning, when you woke up here, through the looking glass, as it were. I know you're not still asleep because we're talking now, and that's way too metaphysical to be happening in a dream. You wake up, I go away. That's just how it works."

Having understood almost half of what had just been said, Marty spoke up. "Well, how has this happened then?" He was as worried about this question as he was about the answer he would receive.

"Hell, I have no idea. Maybe the planets were in alignment. Maybe someone spiked your drink last night. Maybe God got bored and decided to shake things up a bit. The long and short of it is that you've woken up on my side of the fence, and from the looks of your shoulder, you got up on the wrong side of the bed." Mirror Marty made a faux sympathetic face. "Interesting. Normally you can't get injured in a dream, but since you woke up here…" he winced theatrically, "…oh, that's gotta hurt."

Marty tried to compose himself. He was not particularly enjoying the attitude he was giving himself here.

"OK, let's say for a second I believe that all this is happening."

"It is."

"Yes, fine, so how do I get back to my own life?"

That was the big question, and it was one that seemed to rob Mirror Marty of his increasingly irritating smugness.

"Oh, well now, you see, that puts me in a bit of a difficult situation." The smile had retreated completely, and now Marty's reflection regarded him with a guarded caution that seemed to turn the air between them cold. Mirror Marty appeared to visibly shrink within the confines of the mirror as though he had taken a few steps back, and for the first time in their brief interaction, there was a flash of panic and a dark sense of purpose behind those reflected blue eyes.

Awkward moments passed, and Marty stiffened. There was electricity in the air, and Mirror Marty seemed to be shrinking further into the framed distance.

"Listen, if you know how I can get back, you need to tell me. I mean, you're me aren't you?"

The reflected figure straightened. Indignant and suddenly defiant, his words were suddenly desperate. "I'm the you who has danced on rainbows, the you who has dueled with leviathans, the you who has skated across the heavens. You'll forgive me if I'm not particularly interested in going back into the box in your head." There was fire in those eyes now.

Rising shakily to his feet, Marty realized he needed to choose his words carefully if he was ever to get out of this mess.

"Excuse me. I couldn't help but, erm, eavesdrop."

The squeaky, gravelly voice punctuated the silence like someone breaking wind in a Mexican standoff.

Two sets of eyes belonging to Marty darted towards Timbers, but it was the reflection who moved first, looming imposingly within the mirror's frame. His face was wild and desperate, with his arms, outstretched in front of him. He seemed to be lunging for his real counterpart on the other side of the mirror.

In the moment that it seemed as though Marty would be unceremoniously shoved over by his own Id, however, the reflected hands appeared to hit something solid. The mirror's pane. The frame jolted impossibly, and then clattered back against the wall.

"I'm not going back. I'm staying!" bellowed Mirror Marty, and another *thud* sent the mirror swinging dangerously on its hook as a second charge was delivered to the inside of the pane.

Marty, seemingly frozen to the spot for what felt like an age, sprang forward with a dawning realization of what was happening. He grabbed the mirror by its frame, pushing it back against the wall with a crash that he was afraid, for a moment, would send him diving through into the arms of his reflection. On the other side, his teeth gritted and his arms braced against his side of the frame, Mirror Marty heaved back, eyes bulging with frantic effort.

Pain shot down Marty's arm, and he resisted the urge to retreat and nurse his injured shoulder, pressing still harder, his face now inches from the struggling visage of his mirror self. Their eyes met, and Marty could feel the pain in his shoulder being betrayed in his face. He couldn't keep this up for long. Mirror Marty could see it, too, and he leaned closer.

"I'm off, mate, see ya," he whispered mockingly before

ploughing a shoulder into the mirror pane.

There was a heavy crunch, and the mirror cracked raggedly down the middle. The impact from the other side sent the mirror flailing outwards, and Marty was flung across the hallway, coming to rest where he had crumpled just moments earlier. The mirror followed him, wrenching its hook from the wall and plummeted to the ground.

"I've got it," came a shrill cry from Marty's side, as Timbers flung himself dramatically in the direction of the descending mirror. Time slowed, and Marty blinked, mouth agape as his new ally sailed past him, delivering a battle cry as he did so.

"Arrrrrrrrrrrrrrrrrrrrrrrrrrr!"

Timbers hit the floor in the center of the hallway and rolled, cat-like before springing to his feet and holding his little arms aloft. Marty thought for a second that he could detect a proud grin on the pirate's face as he completed his impossible maneuver before the mirror landed, coming to rest with a splintering crash on top of Timbers.

For a moment or two, there was total silence. *These moments of silence would have to be dealt with,* Marty thought. Nobody ever got anywhere by dithering. He scrambled over to the wreckage of the mirror and hauled the frame to one side.

"Timbers! Are you all right?"

Amidst the chaos beneath the frame, Timbers lay on his back, motionless. Brushing shards of glass aside,

Marty surveyed his stricken comrade. "Come on, Timbers, speak to me."

Timbers once again sat bolt upright, spluttering. "Man overboard," he brayed, "What just happened? Did I get him?"

Peering into a large piece of broken mirror, Marty sighed. "No, looks like he got away."

Timbers grunted. "Well, he didn't seem to want to hang around. Literally. Friend of yours?"

"I suppose you could say that. He said he was my Id, and he seemed to know what the deal was here."

"I see." The little pirate appeared to be amazingly chipper for someone who'd just been flattened by a mirror. "Well, we'd better go and find him then I suppose. Any other mirrors in this place?"

Marty wasn't listening. He was eyeing the large, pointy fragment of mirror that was lodged in Timbers' left leg. "Erm. Are you sure you're all right, Timbers?"

Timbers followed Marty's gaze and let out a startled squeak. "Yowsers! How'd that happen? I don't get hurt. I never get hurt!" His good mood appeared to have momentarily abandoned him.

Marty reached over to assist his new friend. "I don't know. The mirror said I can get hurt here, so maybe you can, too? You have to admit, this does seem to be a bit of an 'all bets are off' kind of situation."

"Don't touch it!" Timbers barked. "I'll do it." He reached out a tiny cloth hand and gingerly prized the shard from his leg, grimacing as he did so. The wound it had created gaped alarmingly, frayed cloth and stuffing poking from the hole in Timbers' leg. Deftly, the doll reached into the pocket of his frock coat and produced a small sewing kit.

"I use this to keep the old outfit looking dapper." He blushed, nimbly threading a needle and setting to work stitching his injured leg. "Please don't tell anyone I sew. It's not really very piratey."

Marty suppressed a chuckle and raised a hand to his mouth to disguise a smirk, clearing his throat as he composed himself. "Your secret's safe with me."

Finishing his work with surprising speed and finesse, Timbers rose to his feet and looked up at Marty. "So, come on, are there any more mirrors in the house?"

Marty's thoughts of the matter at hand flooded back and hit him like a tsunami. Springing to his feet, he was replying even as he turned and sprinted back down the corridor towards his bedroom. "The bathroom!"

The bathroom door swung heavily inwards as Marty came diving through it. On the floor beneath the sink lay a small mirror frame, face down, with jagged pieces of mirror scattered in a circle around it.

"No! He got here first."

Timbers appeared at the door. "Wait for me will you? Little legs eh? And one of them freshly stitched." He panted. "Wow. You're racking up some bad luck with these mirrors, matey."

Shoulders slumped, Marty trudged back into the

bedroom, righted the fallen desk chair and sank into it, deflated. "What now?"

Timbers had followed him out of the bathroom and stood at his feet, stroking his wool stubble thoughtfully.

"So this Id chap, he only appears in mirrors?"

Marty shrugged. "Seems that way. Problem is, I'm all out of mirrors."

Timbers stamped his foot triumphantly. "How about we fill the sink with water? I'd like to see him break that."

Marty was already on his feet and racing back to the bathroom. He had already drawn a pool of water in the sink when Timbers caught up with him. "Anything?"

Marty stared into the sink, blinking and waving his hand over the water. "Hello? Hello? Get back here, you crafty git." His reflection in the water copied his movements and eloquent request to the letter. "It's not working. Maybe it only works with mirrors." Marty huffed, exasperated.

Timbers tutted. "It was a good idea though, wasn't it?" he suggested, nodding supportively.

Marty raised a halfhearted thumbs up and smiled weakly. He seemed to be going nowhere fast, but at least he wasn't alone in all this. Of all the people he would have liked to back him up in a hopeless situation, a two foot talking pirate toy probably wouldn't have even made the list. And yet he was helping, and Marty felt a little better for it. He smiled faintly, remembering all the time he spent with Timbers as a child. It would have blown his mind if the little pirate had been so animated then.

Appearing to sense Marty's mood lift, Timbers brightened. "Come on, we can figure this out. Seems to me that we need more mirrors. Big ones. One this fellow can't take a running jump at." Marty lifted his head, an eyebrow raised. "Timbers, you are a genius."

"What? I am? Well, yes, if you say so." The miniature corsair beamed.

"I need to get dressed, we're going to work."

Timbers' smile vanished. "What? You're joking. I thought this was going to be fun," he grumbled.

Marty was unperturbed. He had a plan, and other than an ill-fated scheme to make vodka ice cream, he'd never had a plan he wanted to pursue with any conviction. Smiling, he drew back the curtains and light exploded into the room, exorcising the shadows that had gone before, and opening up the world outside. A world which Marty had seen a million times before, but had never, ever seen like this.

The sun hung magnificently in a deep azure sky punctuated by impeccably shaped clouds. One, a giant eagle wearing a cowboy hat, another a whale on a pogo stick, and yet another, a rabbit playing the drums. The sky met the ground in a mass of tumbling hills, so green they seemed iridescent as the grass blew in the breeze. Towering over them, and reaching higher than the clouds themselves, were outrageously tall trees. Each one was laden with sparkling points of ethereal light, and Marty could make out lavishly colored birds perched in their soaring peaks.

The hills gave way to a sprawling mass of cityscape, buildings plunging into the sky and seemingly swaying with the same breeze that held the trees in thrall. In the distance, an ominous black cloud cast a menacing shadow across a portion of the city, and lightning stabbed into the ground here and there, in stark contrast to the sunlight surrounding it. Past the city, colossal mountains stood sentry-like, tapering to snowy points almost out of sight in the heavens. And still further past them, the sky seemed to shimmer, as though viewed through a heat haze which made it hard to make out any detail.

Marty was not looking in that direction, though. He had an entirely different destination in mind. Away from the city, and beset by an entirely different shade of blue lay the ocean, rolling metronomically towards the horizon, a glimmering multitude of sweeping depths and crested foam. Before that lay the expanse of multi-colored sails and bobbing shapes that was the harbor. And bordering that, enticing with its gleaming metal and flashing bulbs, was Stellar Island.

"Ooh, shiny." Timbers had climbed up onto the windowsill and had his face pressed up against the glass. He whistled in approval at the sight of the glittering theme park in the distance.

Marty nodded in agreement. "That's where I work. That's where we're going. Saddle up."

"Saddle up?" Timbers turned to Marty and frowned. "I'm a pirate, not a cowboy."

After showering, Marty dressed and was pulling on a pair of socks when he heard the letterbox clatter.

"That had better be birthday cards and checks from anonymous millionaires," he called after Timbers, who had trotted into the hallway to investigate. "I'd better not be dreaming about getting bills."

Timbers reappeared at the bedroom door. "I told you, you're not dreaming. You're awake in a dream. Big difference."

"Let's not get into that again." Marty's eyes shifted to the crumpled paper clutched in the little pirate's hand. "What's that?"

Timbers raised the paper and held it out, presenting it to Marty. It was a flier, depicting smiling children, colorful balloons, and a big top marquee tent. Beneath the picture was a cordial invitation to the Giggletastic Carnival Sideshow Spectacular.

Timbers jumped up and down enthusiastically, meeting Marty's determined gaze and immediately seeming to realize that he wasn't acting very piratey.

"No?" he ventured.

Marty, still caught up in his plan, marched past his pint-sized comrade, grabbing a knapsack that hung on the door as he went. "There's a time and place, Timbers, and right now, I've got to find myself." He paused, much of the bravado disappearing as he turned. "Yes, I know how that sounds."

Timbers, clearly sensing the feeling of purpose and motivation needed to be maintained, gave a nod and thumbs up. "Right you are, chief. To the bus stop."

With the mood restored, the pair made for the front door and out into the world.

Outside, the morning air greeted them, clean and fresh, feeling like a morning does after it has been purged by a heavy storm. The sun, however, was dazzlingly inviting, hinting at the possibility of a beautiful day.

Marty stood at his front door and peered up, and then down the street. It was the same street he had seen a million times before and was filled with the same abject normality it had always boasted. The houses, identically filed in a straight line, stood in silence, their front lawns tidy and unkempt in almost equal measure.

The bus stop was handily situated at the end of the road, and Marty motioned with his head for Timbers to follow. Turning onto the street at the end of the path, neither of them noticed the shadowy figure, lurking behind the fence which skirted the house opposite, which was surprising, as the figure was not really very shadowy at all.

Sporting long white shoes, bright green parachute pants festooned with stars, a blue and red stripey waistcoat, and an alarming shock of bright orange hair, the not so shadowy figure watched as Marty and Timbers made for the end of the street. Glinting, gleeful eyes rested atop an impossibly huge, wickedly toothy grin, and stared out from behind ghoulish white greasepaint and a large, bulbous red nose. He watched the figures grow smaller as they headed into the distance, and tugged playfully at the cluster of balloons clutched in his frilly gloved hand. Suppressing a throaty chuckle, he turned and headed in the opposite direction, hauling a satchel onto his shoulder as he did so. A satchel full almost to bursting with fliers. Fliers bearing the legend: Giggletastic Carnival Sideshow Spectacular.

At the other end of the street, like clockwork, the number twenty-one bus had hoved into view at nine a.m. sharp. As with events leading up to this point however, something seemed a little unusual as it approached the bus stop. At first Marty couldn't tell what it was, but as it came to a stop at the curb in front of them, he found himself staring at the wheels, which hovered a few feet off the ground. He ran his gaze over the bus, just a normal, everyday floating double-decker bus. Shrugging, he glanced down at Timbers.

"What the hell. In for a penny, in for a pound." Pushing the 'doors open' button, he made the one giant leap for mankind into the bus, his tiny swashbuckling companion making a bigger, much more ungainly leap for toy pirate kind behind him.

Inside, the bus was completely deserted. And not just bereft of passengers, the cabin also stood driver-less. Marty stood for a moment, unsure of what to do next, before a voice rang out from the ether.

"*Where to, please?*"

Both Marty and Timbers jumped, startled. Looking

around, Marty could see nobody who could claim ownership of the voice, and yet it had come from the driver's seat.

"*Where to, please?*" It chimed again pleasantly.

Feeling as foolish as he had done talking to a cupboard a short while ago, Marty glanced around before venturing nervously "Erm, Stellar Island please."

"*All righty, one adult and one child to Stellar Island. Two pounds, please.*"

"Hey!" Timbers interrupted indignantly. "I am not a child." He drew his cutlass and waved it redundantly at nobody in particular.

"Shhh!" Marty dropped coins onto the tray beside the driver's seat, raising an eyebrow and waiting for a response. As the coins came to rest, two tickets chattered out of the machine next to the tray, and the voice spoke up once again. "*Thank you. Take a seat, please.*"

Marty winked at the flustered buccaneer at his feet. "I think I'm getting the hang of this."

They took a seat by the door, and the floating bus resumed its physics bending journey, moving off at some speed. It bore right at the sort of rate that would have brought squeals of protest from its wheels had they been on the road.

The street that stretched out in front of them carved a path through a completely decimated portion of the city. Huge chunks had been torn out of the buildings on both sides, and cars littered the tarmac ahead, some of them ablaze. Marty rose from his seat, steadying himself with the handrail as the bus swayed along the uneven street, dodging fallen streetlights and broken, spewing fire hydrants. His eyes widened as he took in the scene. He turned to his little pirate companion, Marty's mouth on a squeaky hinge, which appeared to be attempting to enquire about the apocalyptic street they had just turned into.

Timbers was busily crafting a small paper airplane out of his bus ticket but had lifted his head in time to read the very non subtle requests for clarification on Marty's face.

"What, this? It's always like this down here. If it's not giant monsters it's alien invasions, usually three or four a week on this street. To be honest, we'd have been better going around, but then I'm not driving."

"No, nobody is." Marty, having a few minutes ago felt like he was getting the hang of this, clearly wasn't.

Timbers patted the seat next to him, signaling for Marty to shut up, calm down, and be seated. "Look, it's like this. You dream about a huge monster wrecking your town, it happens here. You dream up aliens raining down lasery naughtiness on the planet…" He motioned out of the window as a large smoldering signpost toppled into the road, causing the bus to swerve violently to avoid it. "All here. Must be a nightmare to clean up, mind you, if you'll pardon the pun."

Marty was nodding vaguely. "Sure, that makes sense," he lied. More fallen masonry littered the road now, and he peered out of the side windows, flinching as something exploded impressively somewhere behind them.

"Look, don't worry," Timbers reassured. "We'll be through it in a minute, obviously providing some massive lizard doesn't stand on us or something."

Sure enough, the end of the street filtered into view through thick, black smoke and swirling embers. The little pirate leaned back in his seat, picking up his half assembled bus ticket paper airplane and smiled. "See? Nothing to worry about."

Marty's furrowed brow suggested otherwise, however, even as the bus made a sharp left into a much safer looking, brightly lit, and mercifully intact tunnel. He was starting to feel like he was in over his head. While having a plan was definitely a good thing, charging full speed at said plan, head down and half-cocked, was not.

"Look, I'm starting to think we should perhaps try and get some help with this. You know, call the authorities of something."

Timbers, who had now finished his airplane and was preparing to throw it, cocked his head to one side, his one good eye regarding Marty doubtfully. "Like who? The police? The army? The League?"

"Who are the League?" Marty interrupted.

"Well, they're actually called the League of Fairly Impressive Super Folk, but nobody calls them that."

Marty chewed his lip. This might actually be a line of enquiry worth pursuing. "Super folk? So they have super powers, then?"

"Well, yes," Timbers declared proudly. "Erm, sort of," he added, less proudly.

"What do you mean, sort of?" Marty had already pictured a seven foot tall, armored gladiator with all sorts of impressive powers and perhaps his own theme music.

"Well, there's the Tea Lady," Timbers mumbled, "but I doubt she'd be of much use."

"No, she doesn't sound it." Marty rubbed his forehead in anticipation of what would surely be imminently onrushing disappointment. "What does she do?"

Timbers, to his credit, tried to dress it up, "Well, she has this shiny tray that she flings about. Oh, and she can shoot hot tea from her eyes."

Marty puffed out his cheeks and shook his head skeptically. "That's not massively helpful."

Timbers was defiant. "Depends if you want a cup of tea."

Marty sighed. "Anyone else?"

"Hmm, well there's Captain Inflato," ventured Timbers after a moment's thought.

Marty brightened. "Well, he sounds more impressive. What does he do?"

"Balloon animals mostly," Timbers replied. "He's good at children's parties, though."

As the bus exited the tunnel, Marty was momentarily relieved to see the previous street's desolate theme was no longer present. The fact they now appeared to be underwater was, however, something of a dark cloud to this particular silver lining.

Impossibly, the interior of the bus did not seem to be leaking or flooding in any way, and appeared, in fact, to be making the same steady progress it had been since they boarded. Outside, all manner of marine flora and fauna were passing the tiny window from which Marty was gawping. Off to the right of the bus lay the sprawling wreck of a ship, and Timbers winced, closing his good eye and mumbling something about Davy Jones.

His face still pressed up against the fogging glass of the window, Marty made the standard stereotypical pirate assumption. "So, water dreams I take it? A bit more your thing, I'm guessing?"

Timbers ceased his mumbling and shook his head indignantly, "Not necessarily, no. People don't dream about going to work do they? It's the same for me. The sea is my office."

Marty hadn't really considered that being a pirate was a job. More of a lifestyle choice, or at a push, a very bold fashion statement, but not really a job, as such.

The bus tilted upwards now and seemed to be picking up speed. A school of dolphins hurtled along beside the window and broke the surface of the water at the same time as the bus, twisting and arcing amidst a surging uprush of spray. As they returned acrobatically to the sea, however, the bus had somehow arrived back on dry land, rediscovering the road, which, when Marty craned to look back through the window, was leading back down and into the crashing waves behind them.

"There, land ho! And you were worried." Timbers beamed.

Marty's thoughts were still on the job at hand. "I'm still worried. Right now, if we call in the cavalry, the most we can expect is a hot beverage and a balloon." He deflated back into his seat in a way that would no doubt have had Captain Inflato shouting, "This sounds like a job for…"

Timbers wagged his finger, however. Seemingly, he hadn't finished.

"I hadn't finished." he declared predictably. "There's also Skyrocket, and he can fly."

Marty raised an eyebrow and snapped his fingers approvingly, "Well, that sounds more like it."

"Only indoors, though."

"Pardon?"

"He can only fly indoors," Timbers repeated. Marty threw his hands up in frustration, "I think we can add him to the 'No' list then. Is that everyone?"

Timbers drummed his fingers on his chin. "The only other one I can think of is the Locust."

Marty was starting to think this whole line of enquiry was a dead end. "What does he do then? Eat everything?"

"No, he just calls himself the Locust. I've no idea what he does, to be honest. He just hangs around with the rest of them. He does have a splendid outfit, though."

Marty stared at Timbers as if waiting for a punchline. The little pirate shifted in his seat, fiddling with a button on his coat.

He looked up and shook his head apologetically. "How about we call them 'Plan B,' then?" Standing up on the seat he was now at eye level with Marty. He drew his tiny cutlass and waved it enthusiastically. "Anyway, you still have me."

Marty smiled, in a world that had blatantly not taken its medication, a fellow could do a lot worse. He nodded and produced a semi-convincing thumbs up in support of his swashbuckling companion.

"Anyway," Timbers continued, "we already have all the help we'll need. This funfair, it's next to the harbor isn't it?"

Marty began to nod in the affirmative when a bullet ricocheted noisily off the window frame beside him. Startled, he stopped nodding and started ducking. Outside, what had once been ocean was now dusty plains, punctuated here and there by outrageously tall cacti standing to attention, their prickly hands raised. The street wasn't so much a street as it was a rutted, sunbaked furrow that ran parallel to a railway track. Another gunshot rang out, but this time the squealing ricochet came from a source away from the bus. That source suddenly came galloping past the window.

In keeping with the feel of this new street which they were traversing, Marty fully expected to see a figure in a Stetson, chaps, and spurs come *yeehawing* into view, and was therefore quite surprised when a medieval knight, fully resplendent in gleaming armor, drew level with the window.

The knight carried a sturdy looking iron shield, and

judging from the small dents on its surface, it had been the source of the earlier ricochet. As if to confirm this, three more shots rang out, two of them whistling past the knight's helmet, the third hitting the shield again and *screeching* off at an angle. From behind the bus, a character much more befitting of the scenery hoved into view.

Dressed in blue denims and a long brown duster coat which trailed out behind the horse he was riding, the cowboy was aiming a heavy caliber revolver, eyes trained on his target from beneath a large tan, ten gallon hat. Another shot rang out, the bullet hitting the window at an angle and sending ragged cracks across its pane.

Marty stepped back and once again steadied himself on the handrail. He glanced at Timbers, who stood up on the seat and was observing the chase with enthusiasm. He chuckled and drew the tiny flintlock pistol from his belt, pointing it theatrically at the window and making several "*Pow!*" noises as he did so.

"Cowboys." He snorted, and rolled his good eye at Marty. "Not a very good shot this one, is he?"

It was hard to disagree, since the knight had now passed the bus and was making good his escape towards a small forest that loomed ahead. Another bullet failed to find its target as the shield once again came to the rescue of the fleeing man at arms.

Marty was back at the window again, watching the pursuit quizzically, just as the cowboy stampeded past, leaving a trail of dust in his wake and loosing another volley of bullets in the direction of his quickly departing quarry.

"Hang on. Why is he chasing a knight? The cowboy I get, I mean he looks like he belongs here, but the knight?"

Timbers shrugged. "They don't always keep to their streets. And anyway, they're part of a dream aren't they? I'm surprised they didn't come past on pogo sticks."

Ahead, the rutted trail ended at a crossroads, with three much more reassuringly normal tarmac streets stretching off from it. The street opposite disappeared into the forest, which the knight had sped into only moments earlier, and his pursuer barely slowed as he bolted through the intersection and vanished behind the tree line.

To the left, the sky was visibly darker and ominous clouds rumbled deeply in the distance. Where there was once plains and tumbleweed, there was now dark, featureless buildings lurking on both sides of an unlit street. At the entrance to the street stood a large, rusty signpost, and Marty squinted to make out the lettering upon it through the ever-descending gloom outside. In fact, not only was it getting darker, but he also noticed strong gusts of wind were buffeting the bus, and hurling sheets of newly falling rain at the window. Although the rain had reduced visibility outside, Marty could make out large white letters on a green background. Clearly at some point the sign had read 'Downtown' but someone had crossed out the 'D' with spray paint, and added a 'CL' in its place.

Timbers' voice was suddenly sharp and deliberate. "We're not going that way, no sir."

Marty turned and was met by a look of nervous

caution from his little compatriot. He was staring past Marty and out of the window at the signpost and what lay beyond it. Shuddering, he waved a dismissive hand. "We're going the other way, there's no grinning, squeaky-nosed freaks the other way."

Marty stared back out into the gloom, towards the foreboding signpost. Admittedly, that way didn't look particularly inviting, and yet he was still curious. "Why? What's that way?"

"Look, there's no easy way of saying this without it sounding like a line from a really shoddy action movie." Timbers sighed, cringing. "Back that way are your worst nightmares."

Marty allowed a short chuckle to escape, which he cut short upon noticing the solemn, serious look on Timbers' face. As solemn and serious as a toy pirate is able to look, of course.

Marty patted the miniature buccaneer's shoulder and gestured out of the front windows. The bus was turning right. "Look. See? Calm yourself, we're not going that way."

Timbers brightened, and almost immediately after the bus swung away from the imposing signpost, so did the day outside the window. The wind and rain stopped and sunlight found its way back into the sky. Up ahead, the cries of seagulls could be heard, and the air carried the unmistakable scent of the sea. The buildings on either side gradually became sparser and further apart, and Marty could already see the bobbing masts of boats moored at the harbor. A little way past them and they would be at the gates of Stellar Island and perhaps he could get some answers. Timbers had risen from his seat and was trotting down the aisle to the front of the bus.

He called back over his shoulder. "Come on, we're getting off here."

"But we're going to the theme park. Remember? My plan."

His good eye glinting knowingly, Timbers beckoned for Marty to follow him. "You said you wanted to find help, right?"

The harbor housed several dozen boats of all shapes and sizes, and was surrounded by dry docks and warehouses. The entrance followed a long concrete jetty that plunged out into the bay, with smaller, wooden jetties branching out on either side from which the various craft were moored.

Timbers marched grandly along the concrete outcrop, periodically glancing behind him to make sure Marty was still there, and to nod, wink, or smirk smugly. He was clearly enjoying himself and obviously had a very deliberate reason for being here. Since the harbor neighbored their originally intended destination of Stellar Island, however, Marty saw no harm in humoring his newfound partner, especially since it had been implied that this might be a useful detour.

Reaching the end of the jetty, Timbers spun ninety

degrees and headed down a set of wooden steps towards a line of boats at the waterline. These were the vessels closest to the dry docks, and were bigger and more impressive than those that had weighed anchor on the other side of the concourse.

There, at the end of the wooden gantry, looming over them as they approached, was the largest boat in the harbor. It was a huge wooden galleon, replete with towering masts and billowing sails. Along the side, six cannons poked out from hatches in the hull, and around the deck, ornately carved handrails swept upwards to a raised stern where a large, polished oak wheel stood proudly. The edges of the ship sported elaborate carvings of figures fixed in a lifting pose, as though they were holding up the deck above them, and a large slatted window beneath the stern betrayed glimpses of what appeared to be the captain's quarters behind lavish, crimson curtains. High up amid the masts, two crow's nests sat perched, and emblazoned upon the sails beneath them was the familiar skull and bones motif. Slightly out of place, but most prominent at the center of the ship was a mast, much larger than the others. Thicker and higher, its peak formed a 'T' shape, and it carried no sail beneath it.

Marty stood for a moment, suitably impressed at the sight of the mighty vessel before him. "Is this yours Timbers? Is this your boat?"

Timbers beamed proudly and rocked back on his heels, nodding. "She is indeed," he sang, waving his hand in the direction of a black and gold embossed plaque framed on the bow, depicting the name of ship.

"This, my friend, is the Flying Fathom."

A long gang plank led from the dockside to the deck, and Timbers motioned for Marty to follow him as he ascended. The wood creaked and complained under his weight, having seemingly been designed specifically for tiny pirate weight. Mercifully though it held firm long enough for the pair to board safely.

The slatted wooden deck was very much how one would expect a pirate ship to look. Barrels and crates were stacked here and there, and rigging swayed with the billowing sails. Aside from this, however, the ship appeared to be deserted. The only sounds came from the creaking of the wooden masts, the distant call of circling seagulls, and the hypnotic lapping of the waves against the hull. A shrill, piercing whistle suddenly joined these ambient noises, completely ruining what had been a very calm and relaxing vibe, and Marty's head jerked in the direction of the jarring chord.

As quickly as it started, the sound ceased. Timbers lowered the small tin whistle he had been blowing furiously into. He smiled up at Marty, who was still wide-eyed and startled from the sudden intrusion of decibels.

"Help is here. What's a captain without a crew, eh?" The little pirate turned towards the large wooden doors set into the raised stern of the ship and raised his tiny voice. "Captain on deck!"

Sounds of muted commotion and pattering footsteps issued from behind the door, which proceeded to fly outward as four figures trooped onto the deck and lined up in front of Timbers.

The first figure snapped off a sharp salute and stepped forward. No bigger than Timbers, and similarly stitched, he sported a spotted bandana, but no trademark pirate eye patch. Instead, two beady eyes glinted and a wickedly cheeky grin lit up a surprisingly un-bearded sack cloth face. A black and white striped shirt was crisscrossed by two bandoliers, heavy laden with tiny brass bullets, and black pantaloons tapered into a pair of impressively shiny cavalier boots, almost as fancy as the ones belonging to his captain. A wide funneled blunderbuss hung from a holster on his back.

Timbers stepped forward, turning towards Marty as he did. "Allow me to present my crew. This fine fellow is my right hand man. Goes by the name of Whipstaff."

Whipstaff shot Marty a wide friendly grin, which was lit by a couple of gold (or at least gold-colored) teeth. He nodded a greeting before redirecting his attention to Timbers.

"Been off fighting without us have you, sir?" he chirped in a squeaky, gravelly voice which, it would appear, was quite common amongst talking toy pirates, and pointed a dirty cloth finger at the wound Timbers had stitched not so long ago.

Casting a brief 'Don't tell anyone I sew!' glance at Marty, Timbers cleared his throat theatrically and pulled his frock coat together to obscure the offending embroidery. "Yes, well, we came past Cl...erm, Downtown on the way here."

Whipstaff's eyes darkened, and his smile was replaced by a fleeting grimace, but only momentarily. Beaming again as widely as ever, he slapped Timbers heartily on the shoulder. "Well, at least you got here in one piece."

They exchanged sufficiently piratey growls and guffaws before Timbers moved to the second figure in the line, who towered over his captain at what must have been a good three feet tall. He was barrel-chested, with thick, sack cloth arms. Two of them. Since he was wearing a leather waistcoat, the arms were bare, and boasted several mock tattoos, most prominently a ship's anchor across his right forearm. Instead of cavalier boots, he was wearing what appeared to be wooden clogs and a pair of tattered and frayed tan trousers that seemed a little on the small side. Rather than carry a pistol or cutlass, the tiny giant grasped a ridiculously oversized wooden mallet in his bear paw of a right hand.

"And this is Oaf," Timbers declared. "He doesn't talk much, but he's very handy to have around when you're in a scrape."

He winked fondly at his lumbering crewmate, who reached up to scratch his hatless head, ruffling a thick wooly thatch of blonde hair, before smiling and delivering a large cloth handed thumbs up in return.

Oaf's voice was not squeaky, and luckily so as, relatively

large as he was, he would have sounded rather ridiculous. "Welcome back, Captain," he rumbled gruffly.

Marty's attention turned to the last two crewmates in the line. Aside from the fact that one wore a red headscarf and the other blue, they were totally identical. Both were skinny and seemingly made from the same material as the rest of their merry band. Both wore ill-fitting white linen shirts, which laced up at the collar. Both carried boarding axes that hung from brown leather belts, proportionately way too thick for their owners. And although the pair wore identical patchwork trousers, neither had a shoe between them. They stood barefoot on the deck.

Timbers ushered Marty over to the doppelgangers, stopping in front of the red headscarfed one. "This is Bob." He turned to the blue headscarfed one. "And this is Also Bob."

"Pleased to meet you," the pair chimed in unison.

Marty's brow furrowed as two identical, toothy grins were fired back at him. He raised a hesitant hand in a confused half wave. "Doesn't that make it a bit difficult to tell them apart?" He whispered to Timbers.

The pint sized captain looked up at Marty quizzically. "Well, no." He pointed slowly and deliberately first at one, and then the other lookalike. "Bob…Also Bob. See?"

Marty wasn't sure that he did, but smiled and nodded, anyway. Timbers was grinning at him with no small degree of enthusiasm, and he didn't want to put a damper on things. Enthusiasm intact, Timbers scurried up to the raised quarterdeck and turned to address his crew, now heavy one additional member. "Listen up, me hearties, we've been too long at port, and we've got a new shipmate that needs a ride. Man your stations, and let's get the Fathom underway!"

The crew immediately flew into a flurry of activity. Oaf had set down his mallet and hoisted the anchor, effortlessly reeling the huge iron weight out of the water without the need for a pulley or ratchet. Whipstaff was raising the gangplank and, obviously happy to be setting sail again, appeared to be singing some kind of pirate ditty. Bob and Also Bob had taken a mast each and were clambering up to the lofty heights of the crow's nests that topped the ship. Timbers surveyed the unfolding scene, arms folded and head nodding vaguely in approval, yet he made no motion towards the large wooden steering wheel that formed the centerpiece of the quarterdeck.

Unable to resist, Marty moved behind it, grasping two of the handles firmly. "So, are you going to let me drive, then?" he beamed hopefully.

Timbers turned to face his companion and immediately attempted to stifle a grin, which somehow managed to find its way out as a muffled giggle. Composing himself, he waved a consenting hand. "Give it a try."

Marty attempted to spin the wheel, but it was stuck fast. He tried again, but it would not budge. It was then that he noticed that the whole wheel was made up of one single piece of wood, and seemed to be little more than ornamental. Marty cocked his head, checking for secret panels, hidden dials or switches helpfully marked '*Go*' but there were none to be found. "I don't get it, how do you steer this thing?"

Timbers winked his good eye and once again took the tin whistle from his coat. "You might want to hold onto something," he suggested as he hopped onto a barrel and took a deep breath. This time, three sharp blasts sliced through the sea air, instead of the one long report which had summoned the crew.

Marty was aware that he still firmly grasped the wheel, and his grip tightened as a deafening roar rang out, scattering seagulls from their perches in the rigging, and causing the deck to shudder and shake. It was a metallic sound, a mechanical sound, not dissimilar to the sound a jet plane might make if it happened to be flying at full speed through a gong factory. Just as the noise subsided, Marty was buffeted by a heavy gust of wind. Another followed, and then another, almost rhythmically. The sails billowed as the mighty gusts continued, and he could see that the blasts were coming from the direction of the covered dry docks that ran parallel to the ship. A new, grinding noise now replaced the mechanical roar and seemed to be sounding in time with the wind coming from the dry dock. Marty glanced over at Timbers, who appeared to be saying something, although his words were lost in the maelstrom of noise. He still had an enthusiastic grin on his face and pointed over at the dry dock. Marty turned his attention back to it, just as something huge soared out from beneath the roofed structure and shot into the air above them, causing the boat to sway in its wake.

Marty squinted upwards, struggling to get a glimpse of what had nearly broadsided them. Whatever it was, it was banking overhead and seemed to be heading earthwards at a rate of knots. Just as Marty was beginning to weigh up his 'Man Overboard' options, he was hit by a terrific downdraft, almost falling to his knees under the force of it. Whatever this flying gong factory was, it had slowed its descent and was now perched atop the Flying Fathom. Indeed, perched appeared to be a very apt way of putting it, as Marty peered past the sails, agog at the sight of an enormous mechanical parrot.

Towering over the Flying Fathom, the bird sat atop the large sail-less mast at the center of the ship, which when viewed in this context, was obviously a giant perch. It appeared to be made up of a sort of patchwork of tin, iron, and various other metals, giving it the appearance of metallic feathers. From its head, two huge dazzling white eyes peered back at Marty like twin spotlights. From the gleaming curved beak that they rested above came another jet-gong *squawk*. It cocked its head and flexed its massive steel plated claws, scoring its already heavily scraped and battered perch.

From their nearby posts in the flanking crow's nests, Bob and Also Bob were whooping and cheering, and from the deck below, Whipstaff and Oaf joined in the chorus of approval at the dramatic landing.

Timbers jumped from the barrel and ambled over to Marty, who was still breathing heavily and supporting himself against the wheel. He gave Marty's leg a playful punch and looked up at the giant bird.

"Phew! Zeph's frisky today." He snapped his fingers and turned. "I'm sorry. I've introduced everyone except the ship's parrot, haven't I? Marty, this is Zephyr," he declared proudly.

Zephyr shined impressively in the mid-morning sun, and Marty stared in awe at this complex array of glittering metal. "Magnificent," he murmured, now satisfied that it wasn't, in fact, about to kill them all.

Timbers brought Marty's attention back down to tiny pirate level with a theatrical clearing of his throat. "Help enough for you?" The look on Marty's face fell somewhere between gratitude and awe, and was enough to widen Timbers' grin still further, having provided all the response he needed. "Right you are, then. Course and heading, sir?"

Marty returned fire with a smile almost as wide, and for the first time that day, actually meant it. He motioned towards the neighboring lights of Stellar Island and, almost as soon he did, he could see Bob in his lofty crow's nest making similar motions towards the giant parrot that shared his perch, high up in the rigging.

Zephyr let out another ear shattering call and unfurled his mighty metallic wings, shaking them at first as if in preparation, and then with a whooshing downdraft, put them into action. His whole body pointed upwards, the colossal bird maintained a firm grip on his perch, and all at once, the Flying Fathom was heaving, groaning, and lifting as the wings beat harder and faster. Rising into the air, the Fathom trailed sea water and twisted far more gracefully than a ninety foot galleon had any right to. It pitched to the right, swaying and listing beneath its imposing courier. Marty clutched the wheel once again to steady himself and craned his neck to peer over the edge of the deck at the fast retreating waterline. The boats that had sat alongside the Fathom grew smaller and more remote as more rushing downdrafts filled the air.

Casting his gaze across the deck, Marty could see Oaf and Whipstaff to-ing and fro-ing across the deck, clearly having flown skull and bones airlines many times before. Behind him, at the stern of the ship, Timbers stood, hands defiantly on hips, surveying the receding docks and casting his good eye towards the looming theme park which hung gloriously on the horizon.

At that moment, Marty could not see the patched up, pint sized toy he had dragged along to Kindergarten every single day of his formative years. At that moment, he could only see the captain of a ship and an ally. A friend in a world that still flatly refused to play nice. Timbers glanced back at Marty. He had drawn his cutlass and was waving it enthusiastically, as one rightly should when something undeniably awesome is occurring. As their eyes met, Timbers' grin was as wide and as gleeful as ever, and for the first time since he had woken up that morning, Marty felt a sense that things were going to be all right. He smiled, as much to himself as to the beaming captain in front of him, and aimed a salute at the new friend his old friend had become.

The Fathom turned to face the theme park, sweeping in a wide arc across the bay as it picked up speed, Zephyr soaring like an enormous silver bullet above them. As the ship reached the edge of the bay it tilted upwards, and Marty could see the giant bird angling towards the heavens. The ship rose higher and higher, the once looming contortions of metal, which made up the loops and dips of Stellar Islands sprawling rollercoasters, almost fading out of sight as Zephyr shot vertically into the bright morning sky. And then, as quickly as they had risen to such a supremely elevated peak amongst the clouds, they were diving, hurtling earthwards, and Marty was clinging to the wheel again as the wind screamed in his ears and the Fathom plummeted towards the speck of a theme park below. Zephyr arrowed through the ether like a shaft of silver lightning, and Marty eyed the bulging sails of the Fathom nervously, half expecting the masts of the mighty galleon to snap like kindling. The masts and the sails stood fast, however, and soon he could make out details on the ground below as Stellar Island loomed impressively below them.

At ground level, the descending Fathom, borne by its mechanical behemoth presented an equally awe inspiring site, although oddly, only one theme park patron was present to witness the imminent landing.

From beside a hotdog stand, at the far end of the

park's concourse, one pair of eyes bore witness to the Flying Fathom's arrival on Stellar Island. A large, bulging, manically gleeful pair of eyes that rested atop a fire engine red nose and a wicked, impossibly wide grin. A pair of frilly gloved hands rubbed together expectantly. As they did, a yellow balloon weaved upwards into the sky, a single escapee from a clutch of its brethren, which bobbed and jostled each other above the vibrantly psychotic figure. As the figure sank back into the shadows, a muffled giggle chased the balloon into the midday sky, piercing the silence of what should have been the hustle and bustle of a busy and thriving theme park thoroughfare.

From high above, Marty spotted the single yellow balloon rising from the main street that ran through Stellar Island. Looking past it, he could see no movement. No park patrons. No excited children. No staff dressed in colorful costumes. No cars rattling and shunting amidst the shimmering and flashing lights of the Epsilon Crasher and the Massive Dynamo.

Stellar Island stood empty.

With a serenity and ease that would surely never come from being deposited back on terra firma by a giant mechanical parrot, the Flying Fathom came to rest near the edge of a large natural lake, which formed the center of Stellar Island. Zephyr stood almost motionless on his perch, only moving to stretch his claws and quizzically twist his giant metallic head to view his surroundings.

As the Fathom drifted towards the edge of the lake, Marty rose from his sprawled crash position with a whole new understanding of the term 'all hands on deck.' Around him, the crew was busy with preparations to disembark. Oaf and Whipstaff staggered past, lugging a sizeable gangplank between them, although it was clear Oaf was doing most of the lugging. Bob and Also Bob still sat in their respective crows nests, the former studying the shoreline intently, and the latter involved in some form of communication with Zephyr, still towering over them on his perch. Marty watched as Bob made a slight nod, which in turn drew a sweeping, pointing motion from Also Bob. Immediately as he did so, the giant bird looming over them craned in the direction that his tiny ship mate pointed, leaning visibly and causing the perch to groan and creak under his shifted weight. The deck tilted and pitched, once again betraying Marty's lack of sea legs as he made another grab for the steering wheel fixed to the center of the quarterdeck. The boat was indeed listing to one side. The side, in fact, that Also Bob had pointed at, and that Zephyr had leaned towards.

Marty steadied himself at the helm and smiled. Timbers wasn't kidding, they really didn't need this huge wooden wheel to steer the ship. No, they had a colossal mechanical parrot to do that for them. Even so, he allowed himself to get caught up in the moment as the boat angled gracefully towards the shore. When he had woken that morning, he had not expected to be going into work, and he had certainly not expected to be arriving at work at the helm of a pirate galleon, with a small army of stuffed toys and a massive robotic bird. Even as insane as that concept sounded in his head, it sure beat taking the bus.

Marty's smile evolved into a short snigger. Hell, even taking the bus this morning had beaten taking the bus any other day.

Timbers appeared at the short flight of steps leading down from the quarterdeck as the Fathom came to rest beside a rickety wooden jetty which reached out from the shoreline. The rest of the crew assembled behind him.

"Ready to disembark?" he asked, already trotting down the steps and heading for the gangplank. Marty relaxed his grip on the steering wheel and headed after the band of pint sized cutthroats, catching up to them in a few strides. From behind them, Zephyr let out another ear splitting squawk, and Marty glanced over his shoulder to see the giant bird settling on his perch, his giant spotlight eyes dimming, and then closing altogether.

With the sleeping bird now silent, Marty was struck with how eerily quiet Stellar Island was. It must have been approaching midday by now, and normally the place would have been teeming with gleefully screaming children, adrenaline fuelled thrill seekers, and brightly costumed park employees, not to mention the cheery jingle of fairground music and the thunderous rumble of passing coaster cars overhead. Hopping off the end of the gangplank, Marty assessed the scene, scrambling up the bank from the shoreline to get a better view.

Since Marty's job mostly involved him dispensing tickets at the entrance to the park, it took a few moments for him to get his bearings. Stellar Park was massive, even the real Stellar Park with its coasters and Ferris wheels, its grand concourse, which boasted shops and stalls of all kinds, and its cable car track, so large it skirted the entire island. As vast as it was, though, Marty was aware of his surroundings, having worked there for some years, and with friends in such lofty vocations as the Quantum Singularity Pie Stand and the photo booth outside the Space Gerbils Wacky Hour theater tent. He climbed onto the pathway, which surrounded the lake, and gazed inwards, into the park. Timbers appeared at his side, also looking inwards, likely with no idea what he was looking at or for.

"What are we looking at…or for?" he ventured, after some serious scrutiny.

Marty scanned the rows of attractions and stalls stretched out ahead of him before pointing at a large building nestled amongst various hot dog stands and candy stalls on the right hand side of the thoroughfare. It was jet black, and jutted out of the ground like an obsidian stalagmite. Over the equally black double doors hung a sign that read 'Parallel Hall of Mirrorverse.'

Marty glanced over at Timbers and winked knowingly. Timbers snapped his fingers and punched the air, delivering a triumphant, "Arrrrrr!" They both made a beeline for the obsidian building, with the crew of the Fathom not far behind.

From the other side of the worryingly empty main street, which flowed like an artery through Stellar Island, two eyes watched Marty and the crew of the Fathom as they strode, and in some cases scuttled, purposefully down the main thoroughfare. A lone figure peered out from the shadows of a concession stand, motionless as the group passed and approached the Parallel Hall of Mirrorverse. The eyes narrowed as Marty and his companions ascended the short flight of steps to a high-arched entrance, pushed open the doors and disappeared inside. As the park settled back into eerie silence, the solitary onlooker emerged from the shadows and crossed the street without a sound, ascending the short flight of steps with those steady eyes fixed on the door that had closed moments earlier.

The large entrance hall where Marty and his companions found themselves in was garishly lit and appeared to be a gift shop of sorts. Racks and shelves formed several small aisles in the center of the room, with everything from Stellar Island mugs to tea towels to Harvey the Space Beagle stuffed toys lined up neatly from wall to wall. In the corner, by the register, a sizeable bunch of silver balloons hung, glittering in the reflected beam of a spotlight beneath, and flanking the register on the other side was a full size version of the park's canine mascot. The space suited dog grinned amiably from within a large fishbowl helmet. Marty half expected Harvey to turn and face him, wink and start talking. Hell, pretty much everything else had done that so far today.

As they passed the aisle filled with stuffed toys, Marty paused, removed a miniature Space Beagle toy from the shelf and eyed it suspiciously. The same glassy eyes and cheerful smile looked back at him, but no surprise introduction was forthcoming.

"Hey, Timbers," Marty half-whispered, breaking the mausoleum silence that had followed them from the street.

The crew of the Fathom tried on hats in front of a large dress mirror. Whipstaff was parading up and down sporting a wide brimmed sombrero; Oaf had found a woolen bobble hat which just barely stretched over his blonde thatch, while Bob and Also Bob were fighting over an impossibly large top hat. Hearing his name, Timbers turned from the mirror, causing the tiny red propeller which topped the baseball cap he was modelling to spin with a squeak. He smiled sheepishly, removing it and replacing it with his familiar tri-cornered headpiece, before trotting over to where Marty stood, still holding the cuddly Space Beagle.

"How come these guys don't talk like you do?" Marty enquired.

Timbers frowned briefly, before raising an eyebrow matter-of-factly. "That's a toy, Marty."

Marty rolled his eyes and tutted. "Of course. That makes sense." Again, it really didn't. It wasn't important, though, as that wasn't what they were there for. "Come on, Timbers, we're not here to shop." He motioned past the little pirate towards the gift shop exit, which was also the entrance to the hall itself. Timbers whistled softly to his crew, who ditched their amusing headgear and headed to the far end of the room to meet them. At that moment, the door from the street swung cautiously open behind them, stopping Marty and the pirates dead in their tracks. Turning to face the new arrival, Marty could only see a small figure silhouetted in the doorway. His eyes widened as the figure took a few paces forward.

A girl in her early twenties stepped into a pool of light cast by one of the shop's spotlights. Tall by Timbers' standards, but not by Marty's, she seemed slight and unassuming now that she was clearly visible. She was quite pretty, in that 'long blonde hair, big blue eyes' kind of way, and she appeared to fit in with her surroundings, sporting a black and silver Stellar Island staff uniform.

Everyone in the room seemed to hold their breath, except those who had stuffing where their lungs should be. It was Marty who finally spoke.

"Kate?"

Kate worked in the large cable car building outside the entrance to Stellar Island, concerned mainly with ferrying park patrons to and from the main site. She had worked there for as long as Marty had been an employee, and it had taken him a full two weeks to pluck up the courage to ask her out on a date. It had taken him a full two weeks and one night to completely blow that date.

A preoccupation with everything being perfect had led to nothing whatsoever being perfect, and as a result, they had descended into the awkward friend zone, exchanging cursory 'Good Mornings' and furtive glances across the staff canteen. Marty had since tried to make amends by suggesting a second, far less calamitous date, but she had not gotten back to him, and so the sheepish smiles and painful small talk continued.

As Marty explained everything that happened to him so far that day, she sat and nodded noncommittally, absorbing the absolute fried lunacy on a stick he served up. When he finished, she stared blankly, no doubt processing what would have made a whole team of psychiatrists reach for the rubber wallpaper, before finally speaking.

"Okay," she began, "I'm in. Sounds like fun."

Marty blinked, turning to glance at Timbers, who was equally at a loss for any sort of follow up to this definite statement.

"Erm, I haven't actually said what my plan is yet." Marty interjected cautiously.

Kate rose to her feet, looking past Marty towards the entrance to the hall. "You're stuck inside your own dream, which appears to include me and this little pirate midget." Timbers scowled and reached for his cutlass. "And you're trying to track down your own reflection so you can find a way to get back to your real life, yes?" As Marty nodded, she continued. "So, seeing as how I'm only a figment of your imagination made real, and I really don't have anything else to do, what are we waiting for?"

Timbers chuckled, aiming an increasingly trademarked wink at Kate. "Midget jokes aside, I like the cut of this one's jib. She's got some cannonballs."

Marty sighed, the matter at hand was a corridor away and he was eager to get to it. "Fine, let's get moving then." He headed towards the entrance to the hall, past the small table where the crew of the Fathom had struck up a heated poker game, turning to wait for his new companions, which now seemingly included one sort of ex-girlfriend.

Scuttling along behind the determinedly striding humans, Timbers paused alongside the makeshift poker table. "Better head back to the Fathom, lads," he ordered. "Get the kettle on. We won't be long here." The little captain followed after Marty and Kate. The crew of the Fathom dutifully gathered up their cards and headed for the door that led to the street. As they reached it, Also Bob leaned over to his doppelganger. "I would have won that last hand."

Behind them, Marty and Kate crept cautiously into the stifling darkness of the adjourning corridor. There didn't seem to be any light switch, and no light intruded from the gift shop. Marty's hands went involuntarily out in front of him to keep from colliding with any hidden barrier or object that might lie ahead in the blackness. He could hear Kate's breathing beside him, and the faint sound of tiny pirate footfalls behind him. Squinting in the direction of the breathing, he addressed the patch of darkness he imagined contained Kate.

"Are you sure you want to come with us? It's not that I don't appreciate the help, but today has been…unusual, to say the least…" He sensed the approach of several dozen words from his brain that would have certainly turned this question into an awkward ramble if left unchecked, and stopped himself short. A disembodied voice in the darkness replied. "There's nobody else around, the place is deserted. I've been following you since your mechanical budgie dropped you off. At the very least, this could be fun. An adventure, you know?"

Marty thought that he could even detect a smile punctuating the end of that sentence. It was the same cheerful, animated tone that caught his attention when they first met.

"He's not a budgie," a small voice chipped in from behind them.

As they reached the end of what seemed like a mile long corridor due to the darkness and the slow rate of progress, Marty's hands came to rest on the a wooden surface that felt a lot like a door. He searched for a handle, found one and turned it, pushing the door open. Light spilled out into the corridor, betraying the fact that they had, in fact, only traversed a few feet along it.

Timbers spoke again as he caught up with Marty and Kate. "So, once we get hold of this guy. You. *You know*, the other you. What then?"

Marty's plans had traditionally never gotten this far,

and while he felt somewhat on a roll, he also knew he was, to a large degree, winging it from here on in. "Well, we'll just have to persuade him to help, won't we?" He was surprised at how confident he sounded. Encouraged by this, he took a step through the door into the brightly lit room full of *Martys* beyond it.

The main hall was big. Impressively so. From where Marty stood in the entranceway, he could only just make out the other end of the room, and the walls which stretched off towards it boasted dozens of tall, gleaming mirrors. Each mirror ran from floor to ceiling, with some ridiculously contorted, and some sweeping up and over in a concave fashion, creating a mirrored tunnel effect which would no doubt confuse and delight park patrons. Where the mirrors merely gave way to the ceiling, huge pendulous lamps hung, and above them, smaller lights gave the impression of stars twinkling in a perpetual night sky.

From within each of this myriad of mirrors, a Marty stared back into the room, but rather than mimicking the expression of curiosity and slight awe that the room had instilled into the real Marty, the reflected faces peered out from their respective windows with a mixture of surprise and alarm at his sudden arrival.

"What the hell are you doing here?" They all shrieked in unison. Marty was already at the closest mirror with Timbers at his side, the pirate's hand on cutlass hilt. Still in the doorway, Kate was clearly trying to take in the situation as she stared first at Marty, then at his disconnected reflection. He had explained the situation to her back in the gift shop, but when reality actually hit, and turned out to be nothing close to reality at all, it was a little bit harder to swallow, Marty imagined. Her gaze returned to real Marty. His eyes were fixed on his reflection, his jaw set and his expression impressively determined.

"You know what I'm doing here. You scarpered back at the flat, and I still need answers from you."

Without the expected attempts at a witty retort, mirror Marty lunged towards the pane from his side as he had done on their first meeting. Hitting the mirror with considerable force caused it to shudder and contort slightly, but ultimately sent him crashing backwards and into an unceremonious heap on the reflected floor behind him.

Real Marty raised a 'Yes! My plan worked!' smile and pumped the air with his fist. "These are a bit more sizeable, and they're bolted to the wall. You're going nowhere, mate." He leaned closer to the mirror, peering down at his seated reflection. "Not until I've got some answers."

Mirror Marty's eyes betrayed a panic that had not been there before, trapped as he was. "I…I can't. While you're here, I'm here, too," he wailed breathlessly, and scrambled to his feet, glancing frantically left and right before making a run for it, which took him into the adjacent mirror, then the next one, and the next.

Real Marty took off after him, leaving Timbers staring into a mirror that didn't cast the reflections of him, Marty, or Kate, merely showing the empty room around them. Six or seven mirrors down, Marty caught up to his reflection, who was now at a full sprint and approaching the far end of the room. As he did so, he was immediately transferred onto the large distorted mirror that covered the far wall, where he continued his attempted getaway with impossibly thin gangly legs, elongated arms pumping at his sides, and stretched face puffing and gasping for breath. Such a violent and instant change of direction is all well and good if you are a reflection. Not so much if you are the caster of the reflection and have to abide by the laws of physics. Thanks largely therefore to Isaac Newton, Real Marty ran at full speed into the far wall with an echoing *thud* that stopped him dead in his tracks and sent him staggering.

Leaning forward to catch his breath, hands on his knees, Marty watched as mirror Marty's continued retreat took him along the other side of the room, flashing in and out of each mirror he arrived at. He straightened as his reflection grew smaller, approaching the near wall where they had entered. "This is getting us nowhere. Literally. Where do you think you're going to go?"

Mirror Marty reached the near wall and had disappeared off the edge of the mirror to the left of the large double entrance doors. Immediately he reappeared at full gallop on the mirror to the right of the doors, again reaching the corner and transposing himself onto the long side wall where the chase had begun. Standing where he had come to a stop by the far wall, Marty watched as his reflection charged headlong towards him, then past him, and onwards, seemingly oblivious to the fact that his real self had stopped his pursuit.

Timbers and Kate had made it to the far end of the room now, where Marty had gotten his breath back, and was watching himself running mirror laps.

"So…what now?" Timbers asked. "Shall we just wait for him to wear himself out?"

Marty nodded. The only exercise he regularly partook in was running for the bus or to the off license before it shut, so if his reflection was anything like him, they wouldn't have to wait long.

Sure enough, mirror Marty managed another lap and a half before petering out on the far wall where he came to a halt, panting and wheezing. He looked as though he'd been through a taffy puller thanks to the distorted mirror in which he stood.

Marty finally broke the silence as he reached the stretched version of himself. "Now can we talk? You can see there's nowhere for you to go." His voice carried a faint tone of sympathy, and his mirror clone looked up, blinking and disheveled from his exertions, but also apparently surprised by the manner in which he had been addressed.

Nevertheless, as he regained his breath and composure, mirror Marty folded his arms defiantly and shook his head. "I told you, if you leave this place, I'll get filed away in your head again, and I'm not having that," he muttered through gritted teeth.

Timbers shouted from beside Marty. "What's the

difference? It's not like you can go wandering around when Marty is here and you're stuck in a mirror is it?"

The reflection made an impatient looking face. "You don't understand, how could you? Here I get to *be* at least. Whenever he walks past a mirror, I'm there, and it's a damn sight better than just floating around in his noggin, bumping into random thoughts and disgusting impulses." He glanced at Kate and winked. On the real side of the mirror, Marty blushed. His doppelganger did not.

"Besides, *he* won't let you leave anyway," mirror Marty continued, stopping abruptly as though he had imparted too much information.

Marty raised an eyebrow, turning to Timbers and Kate, who shrugged in unison. "Who won't let me leave?"

His reflection retreated back to his folded arms, closed mouth stance, now looking slightly more uncertain and sheepish than he had done moments earlier.

Kate tutted loudly and stepped to the mirror. She had unhooked a post from the rope which ran the length of the room, splitting it down the middle, and was now holding it threateningly as she advanced. Mirror Marty's eyes widened as she raised the pole over her head and swung it in a wide arc towards the pane in which he stood. He leapt sideways and fell ninety degrees into the adjacent mirror, just as Kate brought the pole crashing into the one in which he had been standing moments earlier. With an ear-shattering crash, the mirror exploded into countless pieces. The entire mirror dropped, sending shards of glass skittering across the floor and flinging a sharp ringing echo around the room.

Timbers and Marty stood with eyes and mouths agape as they looked on, first at Kate, and then at the wooden frame where the mirror had stood. Before either of them could snap out of it, Kate was moving again, this time towards the mirror into which mirror Marty had flung himself. He was rising to his feet when he spotted her approaching. Letting out a cry not dissimilar to a seagull with its nether regions on fire, he again made a break for the adjourning mirror, just barely reaching it before the heavy post created another seven years' bad luck.

Kate headed towards the next mirror, and mirror Marty was already scrambling for a way out when his real self stood between them. "What the hell do you think you're doing?" he shouted. "We're here to talk to him, and we can't do that without the mirrors!"

He fully restrained Kate now, hands braced against the post she was holding out in front of her, pushing towards the mirror that housed the cowering mirror Marty. She fixed him with a determined, yet measured look, and in that instant, Marty felt certain she knew what she was doing and that he could, and should, trust her. A barely noticeable nod passed between them and Marty released his grip on the post.

Kate moved to face mirror Marty and hoisted the dangerous end of the post up onto her shoulder. "Listen up, Marty through the Looking Glass, this is what's going to happen next." Her gaze was unwavering and fixed on the figure reflected in the mirror. "You're going to tell my friend here what he wants to know and we're going to leave you be. If you don't, well..." she hefted the post off her shoulder and regarded it casually. "I'm here because he's here, so I really don't have anything better to do than seek out every single mirror in this city and..." she made a mock swinging motion with the post and a dramatic exploding noise for added effect, "No more mirrors, no more playtime for you. Do you see where I'm going with this?" She dropped the end of the post to the floor and leaned on it, moving in closer to the mirror to eyeball the suddenly concerned looking figure within.

Behind them, Timbers prodded Marty's leg and winked up at his companion, beaming as he did so. "I told you I liked this one." He made spherical motions with his hands. "Cannonballs!"

Before he could shake his head disapprovingly, there was a calamitous roar as the far wall of the hall exploded inwards behind them. Marty was thrown to the ground where he joined an equally shell shocked Kate and Timbers. From the crumpled heap on the ground, Marty could see his mirror counterpart transfixed and pointing where the wall had once been. Looking over his shoulder in the direction of the carnage, Marty saw what his mirror self had been pointing at. He saw what caused the explosion, and he saw the reason for the gaunt, terrified expression on his reflection's face.

Even before the dust settled, and as the sound of its

violent arrival into the building still ricocheted around the hall, the manically nightmarish vehicle hoved into view. At first glance, it appeared to be a car of some kind, vintage in design, and not unlike the old mobster cars of the 1920s. Instead of wheels, however, each corner sported what appeared to be a pogo stick, and it was these springy devices that had propelled the car through the wall, and were now causing it to leap, frog-like into the center of the hall. As it came to rest, the doors sprang open, and Timbers was already on his feet and calling to Marty and Kate as the passengers of the vehicle came spilling out. Marty, still stunned from the incendiary entrance of the pogo car, shot a glance over to where his pirate friend was gesticulating wildly.

"Run! It's Peepers," the tiny captain bellowed over the still echoing roar of the leaping Sedan.

The explosion still reverberating around his head would only allow single word answers, as Marty managed a bewildered, "Who?"

Timbers pointed now, both tiny hands cast in the direction of the carnage, which had arrived through the wall. His words were deliberate, fevered, and squeezed through gritted teeth. "Mr....Peepers...is...behind...you!"

Turning back to look behind him, Marty instantly wished he hadn't.

From amidst the rubble, dust and general mayhem that now formed the center of the hall of mirrors, the preposterous vehicle swayed and dipped on its springs as three, four and still more figures jolted with jerky, inhuman movements from both open doors. The question on Marty's mind would surely have been 'How could they all fit into that car?' had his mind not been so preoccupied with the single overriding thought, *Clowns! Lots of clowns! Where is the exit?*

He was already on his feet, following the quickly retreating Timbers and dimly aware of Kate at his side as one more figure slunk out of the car behind him. Mr. Peepers was considerably taller than his clownish cohorts and moved seemingly without any effort into the light, which had poured in through the newly torn hole in the wall. Huge, unblinking eyes stared after the scarpering trio as they reached the exit at the far end of the room, and wickedly sharp and crooked teeth gleamed as the mouth beneath them unhinged and dropped open. As Marty passed the frantically scuttling Timbers and flung open the exit doors, he heard a bowel-quivering shriek that followed them, his heart threatening to outpace his legs as the cry degenerated into a high pitched, shrill giggle before giving way to the sound of several oversized feet flapping heavily on the ground.

Time seemed to slow, and against his better judgment, Marty shot another glance over his shoulder.

Six clownish figures were making their way swiftly and convulsively towards them like drunken marionettes in a washing machine, meeting and passing obstacles as though they weren't there, and gaining on Marty and his retreating party far too quickly. Even as he glanced, Marty could see the grease-painted faces moving into stark clarity as they sprang into closer view. He wished he could move more quickly, somehow change into a higher gear and propel himself and his friends into the relative safety of the park concourse, but his limbs suddenly felt leaden, as though he were running through treacle.

The short corridor, which led to the gift shop, now felt impossibly long, and seemed to stretch out still further as they charged headlong away from their pursuers. Surprisingly keeping pace with his much taller companions, Timbers drew alongside Marty.

"Hey!" the little pirate chirped, in a voice that carried a flippant tone that in no way fit their current fraught situation. "Wouldn't it be awful if one of us fell over now, like you see in movies?"

Marty's already whirling mind started a new spin cycle, and he just barely managed an incredulous double take at the tiny scuttling buccaneer before the distraction nearly caused him to fall over, like you see in movies. Pinwheeling forward, Marty exploded into the gift shop, Kate and Timbers arriving in a more graceful fashion immediately behind him. Clearly there was no time for sprawling in a heap beneath a rack of sunglasses he had just knocked over, so Marty stumbled to his feet as the sound of heavy footfalls and whooping giggles echoed out of the corridor behind them. Mercifully, the door that led out into the park concourse was only a few feet away and still ajar.

Within moments, it had become loudly and violently more ajar and a swift exit was made into the welcoming relief of the midday sun.

They had been in the gloomy semi-darkness of the hall for what seemed like hours, and the dazzling glare of the sun hit Marty like a slap in the face. Blinking and trying to focus, he caught sight of Timbers, already retracing their steps, scuttling back up the center of the concourse towards the lake where they had moored the Fathom. Acting purely on instinct, and with scarcely enough time to catch his breath, Marty took off after his miniature compatriot, snatching up Kate's hand as she stood equally stunned by the sunlight beside him. Soon, they were all in full flight once again, as the entrance to the Parallel Hall of Mirrorverse splintered outwards and half a dozen clowns spilled out into the light of day. Now fully exposed in the broken frame of the doorway, they looked freakish, stunted, and somehow ill-fitting of reality. They carried themselves with jerky, disjointed movements, and every expression that contorted their faces seemed exaggerated to the extreme. Marty observed all of this in one frantic glance over his shoulder as they reached the top of the hill that overlooked the lake. Stopping, gasping for air, and surveying the waters in front of them, Marty eventually spoke.

"Yeah, there was definitely a pirate ship here when we arrived."

The lake that stretched out before them was certainly light one pirate ship.

Timbers had produced a tiny brass telescope from somewhere within his coat and scanned the skies with his good eye.

"I specifically told them *not* to steal the ship. They are all fired!" he ranted, theatrically shaking a fist at the sky.

Marty however, was more concerned with their pursuers, who had spotted them at the top of the hill and were juddering horribly in their direction, whooping and giggling with menace. "We don't have time for this." a voice rang out from his side. It was Kate, and she was already bolting across the edge of the lake towards the adjourning path, beckoning Marty and Timbers to follow. Arriving at the doorway of a huge, stark, featureless building, she waited for the others to catch up.

Marty saw the sign over the door first as he approached. Metallic and shimmering, it proudly declared 'Zero-G Fun House.'

Slowing to a stop alongside Kate, he raised a hand of concern.

"Erm, just to clarify. We're stuck in my dream, we have a bunch of clowns from hell chasing us and we're about to go and hide in a fun house?"

Pausing for the dawning realization, which didn't appear to materialize in his colleagues, Marty continued.

"Do we not think this is, oh, I don't know, a really bad idea?"

Kate clearly didn't. "Do you see anywhere else to hide around here because I don't?" Scanning the burger stands and picnic tables that skirted the lake, Marty realized Kate was right, just as she turned and flung the doors open, disappearing inside. Timbers appeared to second the motion as he scuttled past Marty and into the fun house.

Flinging exasperated hands in the air, Marty shouted after his fleeing compadres. "Brilliant! Where are we hiding next? A basement? A graveyard? An old abandoned mansion? Don't forget to shout 'Hello? Who's there?' just before you get eaten."

Before he could think of any more witty and cutting comments to make, the hellish mob of circus horrors reached the top of the hill. They advanced, filling the air with demented shrieks and whoops. Marty returned fire with a rather ineffective single, strangled yelp. With nowhere else to run, and against his better judgment, he turned tail and followed his companions into the darkness of the fun house.

Flinging open the doors which had, moments earlier given way to Kate and Timbers, Marty bolted inside, planting a foot firmly on absolutely nothing at all. Swan diving head first towards where the floor should have been, he instead performed a wildly flailing somersault, which would have drawn a round of applause from onlookers (had there been any looking on at the time) before eventually reaching terra firma, some two or three meters lower than it rightfully should have been, and also not particularly *firma*.

Disoriented, Marty felt cold, yielding plastic beneath him and gingerly wobbled to his feet. To his right, Kate was steadying herself against the wall, and apparently equally just as unsteady. As Marty was about to enquire about Timbers' whereabouts, he appeared at Kate's left shoulder, before disappearing again behind her. Seconds later he reappeared, an excited grin stretched across his face, before vanishing once more. It wasn't until Timbers' third bounce that Marty realized what they were all standing on. Glancing down, he, too, attempted a cautious bounce on what was indeed a completely inflatable floor. His shoes squeaked and rasped on the plastic, producing a sound that would have drawn muffled giggles from any adolescents who happened to be in the room.

From behind Kate, Timbers giggled. "Someone step on a duck?"

Without even waiting for the indignant reply, which would surely have followed, Timbers sprang from behind Kate. "This is brilliant!" he declared emphatically, coming to a stop, but still bouncing in front of Marty. Catching the little pirate on an ascent, Marty plucked Timbers out of the air, drawing a sharp, "Arr!" of alarm as he did so, before heading unsteadily over to where Kate was propped.

"Why are you so cheerful? You've just been boat-jacked, remember? Oh, and we're being chased by…well you saw them," Marty reminded the struggling corsair in his arms.

Timbers ceased his wriggling and set his jaw defiantly.

"We'll get to them, and we'll get away. Probably. In my experience, you take fun where you can find it. And anyway, I'm a pirate! We're reckless and have no regard for our own personal safety. It's kind of my job to not give a rat's ass."

Marty considered replying, but could find no flaw in the beaming buccaneer's logic.

"Looks like there's a way through over there." Kate pointed to the far end of the wobbly room which tapered and eventually became an equally wobbly looking corridor.

Above them, three dull, booming thuds rang out loudly from the main entrance doors. Two and a half pairs of eyes shot upwards to the source of the knocking, and the leering, jagged voice which issued from the other side of the door shortly afterwards.

"Hello…hello…*hello!*" The final hello was shrieked with such gleeful ferocity, and was followed by such a disjointed torrent of manic, high pitched giggling that it almost ripped the door from its hinges.

Then, the door *was* ripped from its hinges. As it hurtled through the air towards Marty, everything seemed to slow down, leaving him with what seemed like an age to ponder why it was always the dreams about unpleasant things that did this. Things never moved in slow motion when you have suddenly discovered you can fly or have invented an exciting new kind of sandwich. No, it only seemed to give you time to fully absorb and enjoy the many tentacled, slobbering things in the dark or the pointy things that loomed calamitously overhead while you stand rooted to the spot.

Marty realized the reason he was rooted to the spot was because of all this pondering, and threw himself heroically towards Kate, sending her bouncing against the wall as the door plodded past at a pace that made his grand gesture now seem somewhat unnecessary. Splinters hung around it like orbiting satellites as it floated past, spinning and fanning out like some kind of languid shotgun blast.

As shadows fell upon them, Marty remembered why the door was now making its way gradually into the room and glanced upward before grabbing Kate by the hand, Timbers by the leg, and bounding towards the corridor on the far side of the room.

The shadow casters were descending through the air from the torn open doorway, floating downwards, almost in flight, Marty could make out every grease-painted sneer and sinuously contorted (yet brightly clothed) limb. He could see every manically glinting, bulging eyeball, and several rows of wickedly crooked, yellow pointed teeth, which clowns really had no business having.

"Stop gandering and get a move on," Timbers yelped as he dangled upside down from Marty's grasp, clutching his hat to his head with one hand, and struggling to draw his cutlass with the other. As they reached the corridor, Marty risked another glance over his shoulder. The horrific clowns that had glided hideously but nonchalantly to the floor had now landed and were moving, bounding, and darting after them. Jerky and unnatural, whooping and squealing, chuckling and barking. More worryingly, they were moving unerringly quickly, legs and arms flailing like rabid monkeys in a disco. A bouncing cacophony of big top abomination.

Having barely slowed to assess the onrushing carnage, Marty, Kate, and Timbers sprang into the corridor with the carnival from hell mere feet behind them. Pale, gnarled hands grasped at air, which seconds before, had been occupied by two people and a tiny pirate. The floor below dropped into a steep slope after a few vaulting strides, and Marty heard what sounded like a balloon being squeezed as their pursuers jammed into the passageway that was fast becoming more of a chute.

Had the current situation not carried the very real threat of brightly colored, but unspeakably freakish, danger behind them, ricocheting along an inflatable tunnel before suddenly hurtling headlong down a fiercely steep slide might have held some amusement and entertainment for Marty.

Timbers, however, was not so philosophical in his assessment of the level of peril they found themselves in, and signaled his approval of the blow up rollercoaster they were now riding with an enthusiastic, "Yahooooooooooo!" which terminated sharply as the tunnel came to an abrupt end and deposited them like water from a tap into a huge circular chamber.

Thankfully, the room beneath them was as buoyant as the one from which they had fled, making their landing more ungainly than bone crunching. Timbers was first to his feet, straightening his hat and gazing gleefully at the lofty ceiling. "We have *got* to do that again!" he whooped, dusting himself off and bouncing on the spot.

Kate rolled her eyes as she also struggled to stand. "Is he always like this?"

As he scanned for an exit, Marty stopped and almost smiled. "To be honest, before today he was a lot quieter."

Seeing no immediate means of escape, Marty lurched to his feet and turned full circle. Although much bigger than the first room, this mighty arena was equally inflated, its concaved walls forming a vast, padded dome. "Can anyone see a way out?" he asked, "because we're going to have company in about no seconds flat, and we need to not be here."

Marty glanced at the hole in the ceiling. They couldn't be far behind, and he had already come up with one plan today.

Kate stumbled forward a few jaunty steps, grabbing Marty's shoulder for support. "There isn't one. In a dream there doesn't have to be. It doesn't have to make sense, does it?" She sighed. Momentarily distracted by Kate's hand on his shoulder, Marty was caught completely unawares as something small and swift shot past him. Staggering backwards, he squinted at the nimble and distinctly pirate-shaped blur as it sped past, arrowing towards the nearest wall.

Timbers hit the side of the dome at speed and with some force, sending the plastic bulging inwards and holding him briefly in place before Newton's law took over. The tiny buccaneer flew backwards, pinwheeling and skittering across the floor, arriving in an undignified heap at Marty's feet. The wall quivered and shook, emitting a comical sound one might only expect a cartoon spring to make, but remained unbroken.

Struggling to his feet, he darted a sheepish glance at Marty. "Nope, that didn't work." He shrugged.

Glancing up at the hole in the ceiling again, which would surely be filled with white grinning faces at any moment, Kate flung her hands up in frustration and made her own attempt to break through the plastic barrier, failing in an equally spectacular fashion.

"Okay, so now what?" Her voice carried a hint of panic, rising in pitch at the end of the question as the huge floor suddenly lurched sideways.

Knocking the trio off their already unsteady feet, the room continued in what was now a definite clockwise rotation, gaining speed and whirring like a wind turbine. Marty felt himself sliding towards the edge of the dome while the room picked up still more speed. Timbers shot past Marty's head for the second time in as many minutes, albeit unwittingly this time.

The entire chamber spun at a rate that sent Marty pinballing after Timbers, who was pressed face first against the plastic of the dome. Marty crashed into the wall next to him, the sound of the whirring room and muffled pirate complaints filling his ears. Then a new sound joined the chaotic concerto, an awful shrieking, whopping, giggling sound that Marty had heard before. He strained to look up as the hole in the ceiling birthed six cackling freaks into the room below.

The whirling chamber settled into a more pedestrian rotation, and Marty was able to peer backwards over his shoulder as he, Timbers and Kate slid from the wall, arriving back on not-so-solid ground with a slumping half-bounce.

Behind them, the clowns hit the floor and sprang in all directions like so many demented Jack-in-the-boxes. Twisting and contorting impossibly in midair, three of their number had been propelled in the direction of the slumped trio. Marty struggled to his feet but was still finding the motion of the room far too mobile for his liking. He lurched to one side, just as a wickedly taloned hand within a tattered white glove swatted at what would have been his head seconds earlier, and tumbled over to where Timbers had somehow managed to best gravity. The tiny pirate was on his feet, struggling with his cutlass.

The owner of the hand landed feet away and leered over at the pair, crouching as if to pounce while gurgling a throaty chuckle in their direction. Marty froze in its gaze, and Timbers heroically fell on his backside as the tiny sword at his side refused to budge from its sheath. Whooping with demonic delight, the grotesque jester sprang forward, reaching and grasping with its outstretched claws, looming over Marty and Timbers like a vulture swooping down on its lunch.

Marty flinched as a foot shot past his head and planted itself into the leering visage of the onrushing harlequin, connecting with a crunch and a faint *honk* as its bright red nose absorbed the full force of Kate's size six in what must surely have been a display of either a small degree of martial arts skill or a large degree of luck.

The dented clown flew backwards like a rag doll into two of his cohorts, sending them sprawling on the spinning floor, as Marty turned to regard the triumphant Kate. She stood over him with her arms planted firmly on her hips.

"Yeah!" she spat. "I…I can't think of anything witty to say…"

Marty snapped out of the admiring hypnosis, which had momentarily taken him out of the situation, and grabbed Kate's hand. "No need, we've got to move."

To their left, Timbers shrugged. "I'd have gone with, juggle that!' Sweeping him up by his collar, Marty made a break for the far wall, with Timbers still conjuring one-liners. "No, no, I've got a better one. 'This ain't no custard pie.'"

Time again seemed to slow to a crawl, and as they fled, three clowns closed on them, bouncing and shrieking as they gained. Marty felt a hand on his shoulder, and spun. Twisting and falling, he evaded another wickedly hooked haymaker as he half-skidded, half-bounced into the fetal position. A clown shaped figure whipped past him as he fell, and reached for him, missing by inches. Jabbing a foot upwards, Marty connected with something hard and sinuous and heard a shrill squeal as the figure wheeled away, bumping and jarring violently against the ever turning walls.

To Marty's right, Timbers had taken fetal to the next level and was balled up tightly, colliding with a group of ominous figures in front of them, like a swashbuckling bowling ball, which sent them crashing to the rapidly rotating floor. Still they came, springing back to their feet as quickly as they had been knocked off them. Marty and Kate were running out of places to bounce to, while Timbers was now simply whirling in a tight circle, threatening with various colorful pirate expletives to keel haul anyone who came near him.

Two clowns converged on the tiny corsair, and the force of their landing sent him shooting upwards and out of their reach. Unfortunately, this put them within reach of Timbers' companions, and reach they did.

Marty felt a cold, claw-like hand clamp round his ankle. Its owner screeched with manic delight as though it had been fishing and had just gotten a bite. The hand began to reel Marty in, and he flailed backwards with both arms, inadvertently catching a random clown face with one fist, and removing a clump of bright blue hair from a second clown head with the other. Both injured freaks fell like demolished chimney stacks on either side of him, but still Marty skidded backwards, ensnared by the ghostly white, taloned pincer at his feet. Mustering his courage, Marty twisted to face his captor and, with the best battle cry he could manage, drove towards it shoulder first.

The figure, its eyes manic and bulging, let out a gleeful cackle, releasing Marty and spreading its arms wide in beckoning anticipation. Marty ploughed forward, missing his target as it lunged to one side, still chuckling mockingly. It watched as momentum carried Marty onwards and into the hunched shape of another clown which was bearing down on Kate, cornered and flailing at her tormentor. It buckled as Marty inadvertently, but effectively, lifted it off the ground and sent it skittering away.

Kate struggled to her feet on the still spinning floor, and Marty turned from where he had landed, his eyes locking on the looming figure of the braying harlequin he had shot past moments earlier. It slithered forward, squealing with delight and reaching with twisting, grabbing hands. Now towering over Kate and Marty, the giggling jester advanced, grasping and snarling with teeth bared. Had gravity not taken its course, those hands and teeth may have found their mark. It was Timbers, however, on his way back down to earth, who found his target. Landing with a resounding *thud*, the tiny captain dropped feet first onto the unsuspecting head of the ghoulish attacker, who went down like a dirty joke at a formal dinner party.

His mind reeling with simultaneous shock and relief, Marty scrambled to his feet, rocking against the momentum of the room. He grabbed Kate's hand and steadied himself. "If we don't get out of here soon, we're going to run out of luck and incredibly fortuitous Kung Fu moves."

Timbers had arrived at his side, and managed to wrestle his cutlass from its sheath. "Couldn't agree more," he cried, triumphantly holding the miniature sword over his head. "A wise man once said, if in doubt, give it a clout."

Suddenly realizing the intention, Marty's eyes widened. "Who said that?"

Timbers paused, twirling the cutlass in midair. "Me. Just then," he retorted proudly, before driving the blade firmly into the inflated plastic at his feet.

At that moment, the world seemed to explode. A deafening *pop* was followed by a huge rush of air as everything suddenly shrank. Timbers had carved a jagged tear into the floor, and what seemed like a hurricane was now escaping from it. The little captain shot into the air again, meeting the rapidly diminishing ceiling and rebounding off it like a cork from a bottle. Kate and Marty were flung backwards as the room around them imploded loudly and violently.

With the sound of a deflating balloon, which would undoubtedly have drawn sniggers from Timbers, had he not been pinballing from floor to ceiling, the great chamber of the Zero G Fun House shriveled and shrank in on itself, collapsing around clown, human, and toy pirate alike.

Finally everything settled into so much plastic sheeting, with the faint sound of escaping air still issuing from the tear in the floor, leaving several prostrate bumps in what was now no more than a vast groundsheet.

From the hole that Timbers had carved, Marty's head squeezed out into the afternoon sun. He wrestled himself free, pulling Kate out behind him. He glanced here and there for signs of clownish assault, but none was immediately forthcoming, although some of the prostrate bumps were stirring. The one closest to him wriggled and struggled, before a shiny silver blade shot upwards, cleaving a second fissure in what had once been the Zero G Fun House.

Poking his head out of the hole he made, Timbers' one good eye blinked in the bright sunshine. "My plan worked then," he chirped, squirming to his feet.

Kate was first to her feet, running over to where the little pirate stood, and hoisting him up in her arms. "You saved us!" She yelled, laughing and twirling him around.

Timbers seemed momentarily coy. "Please, no more spinning," he implored. She set him down, and he dusted himself off theatrically. "If you want something done right, ask a pirate," he mumbled, his roguish grin rapidly reappearing.

Sighing with relief, Marty shot a wink at his pint sized compadre. "Nice work, captain, now how about we make a move before this Peepers guy gets here to dig his chuckle buddies out?"

Timbers wasn't smiling anymore. He was pointing. "*That* Peepers guy?" A shaky finger pointed past Marty at a shadow watching from the path behind them.

Mr. Peepers stood shrouded in darkness at the brow of the hill above, and seemed to float out into the light as Marty turned to follow the pointing finger. He was indeed noticeably larger than the clowns they had escaped from

THE FORTY FIRST WINK 89

moments ago, although he sported the same devilish grin and insanely bulging eyes. The trio froze as he descended towards them, his gaze cold and hypnotizing, his progress purposeful and impending. As Marty watched, rooted to the spot, a mighty shadow passed over them. Snapped from his trance, he glanced upwards as the looming darkness was joined by a deafening roar and a smothering rush of wind.

The Flying Fathom appeared like the rising sun behind them. It passed overhead and angled in a tight arc, which bought the ship to within meters of the ground. As it swooped in front of Marty and his companions, a rope ladder cascaded from the deck.

Not wishing to become any more acquainted with the leering circus freak closing in on them, Marty lunged for the trailing ladder as it swept past. He caught a handful of rungs and turned to his friends as the Fathom dragged him along.

Before he could say, "Move it! Holding down a floating pirate ship isn't as easy as it sounds," Kate was at his side and already past the first few rungs of the ladder. Marty took larger steps now, bounding, floating steps as the Fathom banked and picked up speed. Timbers had, however, vaulted onto the bottom rung of the ladder and beamed up at his friend.

"Don't tell me you're not having fun," he sang enthusiastically, just as the huge ragged right hand of Mr. Peepers fell onto Marty's shoulder.

The demonic clown was upon them, close enough to

shock Marty into nearly losing his grip on the ladder. With one hand retaining purchase, he wheeled around and was face to face with Mr. Peepers, who craned closer, his grin now impossibly wide and eyes even wider. Marty winced as he caught a face full of hot clown breath.

It smelled like candy floss, Marty thought. Candy floss and terror.

This was quite enough incentive, were any needed in the first place, for Marty to literally get a move on. He shrugged and jolted away from the grease-painted abomination that snared him. Slipping free from its grasp, Marty threw every last ounce of strength he had into the hand which gripped the ladder as he heard a tiny pirate voice above him yell, "Hard to port!"

With that order, the Fathom swung gracefully to the left, lifting Marty upwards and outwards in a wide arc. With eyes closed and one hand clamped firmly onto the bottom rung of the ladder, Marty heard the muffled sound of Timbers complaining about yet more spinning over the *whoosh* of the downdraft from Zephyr's wings and the creak of the tilting and pitching ship. Just as the drama and tension threatened to go on a little too long and become tedious, Marty felt the ladder retracting as it rattled across the edge of the deck and hoisted them towards safety. Finally, the deck was within reach. With his free hand, he dragged himself into an undignified and breathless heap with Timbers arriving in a similar fashion behind him.

The miniature captain sprang to his feet, eyeballing the hoister of the ladder accusingly.

Oaf looked up from said hoisting and winced at Timbers' glare, shifting his feet sheepishly.

Timbers took a step forward, hands defiantly on hips. "Nice of you gentlemen to put in an appearance." He growled. "Now, perhaps you would like to tell me where in Blackbeard's biscuit barrel you scurvy mutineers have been?"

Oaf's bottom lip quivered slightly but before he could speak, Whipstaff stepped out from behind him. "Stay your blade, Captain. We've been looking for you." He patted Oaf on a sizeable forearm, and the tiny giant gave a heavy sigh, nodding in agreement. "When Peepers and his uglies showed up, we set sail to come and get you. Trouble is, when we got back to where we left you it was pretty much rubble and you'd hightailed it. We've been circling ever since, on the lookout." He motioned up into the rigging where Bob and Also Bob were perched in their crow's nests beneath Zephyr's mighty wings. They waved cheerfully back.

The fire fuelling Timbers' tirade subsided. He held an apologetic hand up to Oaf, who was rubbing his own hands anxiously but managed a supportive half-smile in return.

"Well, of course," the captain ventured encouragingly. "I'd expect nothing less from a crew of such fine standing." He held his hands out in approval and shot Marty a sideways glance. He *had* slightly underestimated them, but only for a little while. It was hardly worth mentioning, and his look suggested that he would prefer if Marty didn't.

Marty, however, wasn't paying attention. He was clutching the rail of the deck and peering back at Stellar Island. It was some way below them but still visible from the hovering, stationary Fathom. The ship hung motionless from Zephyr's claws as the giant bird awaited new orders. He turned back to his companions, grimacing with frustration.

"We had him!" Marty shouted, throwing his hands up. "He was so close to talking. Now we've got to start all over again. We need to find a mirror. Are there any on board?"

Timbers shook his head. "We're pirates, Marty. We don't really have much of a makeup routine."

"It's a good thing I do then," Kate interrupted, fishing in her pocket and producing a small round silver case. Walking over to Marty, she placed it in his hand. "Why do you think I was so quick to start smashing mirrors back there? If you're going to bluff, you better make sure you've got an ace up your sleeve." She smiled as Marty looked down at the powder compact case. He pushed the button on its side and it flicked open to reveal a tiny circular mirror on the upper lid. From it, Mirror Marty gazed back at him, a bewildered expression meeting his real reflection's now beaming face.

Marty launched into an impromptu high five, which missed and sent him into an awkward half hug which neither he nor Kate had expected. His face flushed and he quickly retracted the accidental embrace.

"Wow, that's thinking on your feet. Good work," he managed, attempting to take attention away from his blushes with a weak thumbs up.

Glancing furtively at Kate, Marty was surprised to see she had adopted a similar crimson shade, and was for once glad of the untimely interjection of his pirate partner.

"What's that? Is that a mirror?" He was hopping on one foot, trying to get a better view of what Marty held in his hand. "It is. Ha! I told you this girl was a cracker," he declared to his crew.

Smiling again, and back to his normal color, Marty returned his attention to his reflection, who was not smiling. He was pointing. Pointing back over Marty's shoulder with a look of panic.

Marty turned in the direction of the pointing finger just as a dozen brightly colored balloons rose into view at the edge of the deck. They continued their ascent, trailing a cluster of thick string in their wake. As a dawning realization hit Marty, the tapering string pulled a tattered white glove into view. Then an arm. Then a pair of bulging eyes set atop a ragged, manic grin.

Mr. Peepers sailed into full sight before releasing his balloons and dropping to the deck in front of Marty. Giggling and chomping his teeth, the nightmarish clown lunged at Marty with languid, exaggerated movements. Out of sheer instinct for self-preservation, Marty threw his leg out in front of him in what he hoped would result in another accidental martial arts move. Although it appeared to be more like the hokey pokey, it still connected with the advancing Peepers and sent the gibbering freak staggering backwards.

Behind him, Timbers was already delivering orders. "Look lively men, we've got a boarder," he barked. As Peepers steadied and raised his hands menacingly, the little captain had already leapt onto his back, and a tilting brawling mass of clown and pirate lurched its way towards Marty. Amid the frantic howls and gruff cries of, "Avast!" Marty sidestepped and made a grab at the pirouetting chaos. Catching a handful of something, he pulled and fell backwards as Peepers' arm came away from the melee, separated from its owner. Mid-scuffle, Peepers craned his head impossibly to one side to eyeball Marty as he sat clutching the detached arm. Timbers struggled valiantly in the grip of the devilish clown's remaining claw as more of the shrill giggling filled the air.

Peepers, his gaze still locked on Marty, reached and pulled an arm from behind his back. An arm identical to the one Marty was holding, which now filled the void that the other had left. As the new arm flexed and stretched, Marty realized the limb he held was also flexing and stretching, searching for something to grasp, something to capture in its disembodied grip. In a split second, Marty also became aware of movement in his peripheral vision.

Kate lunged for Peepers' blindside where Timbers still dangled, and the lumbering shape of Oaf heaved one of the cannons, which flanked the deck, to bear on the cackling harlequin. The arm that Marty held arched backwards, seeking purchase, and in an instant, he grabbed it at its shoulder and hurled it into the face of his giggling tormentor. It connected with a dull smack and Peepers shrieked as he punched himself squarely in the face. He pinwheeled sideways as a thunderous *boom* shook the deck.

Oaf's cannon rocked wildly backwards as a cannonball screamed towards the stumbling clown. Again, time fell to a maddening crawl as the lead orb streaked across the deck. As it approached its target, Marty felt sure he could see a sneer of knowing contempt take hold of Peepers' nightmarish features as the dreadful clown spun to face the onrushing barrage.

In slow motion, Peepers flung out an oversized foot, which connected with the cannonball, sending it skywards, and bringing time rocketing back to normality with sickening clarity.

Ricocheting upwards through the rigging, the cannonball plunged past the Bobs in their crow's nests, and Zephyr let out a gear grinding *squawk*, letting go of his perch to veer away from the arcing shot.

Now, anyone who has dabbled in physics will tell you, anything that is held in the air by something, even a giant mechanical parrot, has only one direction to turn if it is not held up anymore. Even Marty, who could never lay claim to being a scholar, had a fair idea of what was going to happen next…and he was correct.

Dislodged from its mighty metal bearer, the Flying Fathom dropped like a vast wooden hailstone from the heavens, its passengers clinging desperately to rigging, railings, and each other as they fell.

Peepers however, stood unaffected on the deck, as though detached from the surrounding calamity, the wind whipping around his bright baggy trousers, with Timbers still clutched in his unyielding white claw. From where he crouched, hanging onto the deck railing as the world whipped past him, Marty watched while Peepers' waistcoat billowed and bulged. More garishly colored balloons issued, seemingly from within the still grinning clown, and flew back up into the sky. Peepers caught the trailing strings and laughing balefully as he rose from the plummeting deck and away from the crashing Fathom.

Timbers pounded with tiny cloth fists against the constricting hold of his captor, a string of colorful suggestions as to Peepers' lineage peppering the deafening sound of crashing ship around him, but to no avail. Marty caught a final glimpse of his miniature compatriot as he was carried into the sky, struggling against Peepers' unrelenting grasp. Both clown and pirate rapidly became a giggling, cursing dot above the Fathom, as it hurtled ever downwards.

Dropping out of the clear blue sky, the no longer Flying Fathom lurched and skewed like a hang gliding brontosaurus, sending its passengers skittering across the deck. Marty clung to a section of rigging, the breakfast he had consumed earlier clamoring to make an encore appearance. Across the deck, Oaf was anchored to one of the masts with Whipstaff flailing wildly from one of his lumbering crewmate's giant paws. Above them, the Bobs were braced in their respective crow's nests, only their identical faces visible from the deck below. Marty craned his head, searching for Kate, just as she skidded past him, scrambling for purchase and seizing Marty's outstretched hand to halt her perilous progress.

Hauling her back towards him, Marty tried to focus and to not think about the ground, which was undoubtedly looming fatally below them. In certain death scenarios, it is quite difficult to think of anything other than your own certain death, and yet Marty's whirling montage of thoughts still managed to factor in the image of Timbers' savage clown-napping, as well as a vaguely contented feeling gleaned from a tight embrace with the object of his affections. The latter thought was of course completely inappropriate given their current situation, but had popped up nonetheless.

From high above them, Marty thought he could detect the sound of the Bobs squealing; a high-pitched wail which grew in pitch and intensity. He looked up towards the source of the cry, just as the realization hit that it wasn't the Bobs that were making it.

Arrowing towards the descending Fathom, Zephyr let out another shriek while he swooped down on Marty and his fellow plummeters. As he drew closer to the ship, the mighty bird stretched out his gleaming claws and grasped the central perch-like mast, heaving his huge metallic wings backwards as he did so. The mast groaned and the Fathom's descent slowed, its bow pitching and swinging like a giant pendulum, dislodging Marty from where he had been fastened to the rigging. Both he and Kate slid free of their mooring, coming to a clumsy but merciful halt just short of the edge of the deck. Peering over the side, Marty's eyes widened as the ground came into sharp clarity, looming ominously and way too quickly below them.

He could not see Zephyr, but Marty could feel the colossal parrot fighting to bring the Fathom under control as buffeting gusts of wind sprang down on him in waves from the flapping wings of the laboring bird.

The Fathom tilted sharply sideways, and suddenly a glinting expanse of water was visible beneath them as the ship continued its haphazard descent. It was the ocean, spanning invitingly out from the edge of Stellar Island, reaching out to the harbor in the distance.

Curving in a wide, rakish arc, Zephyr heaved his unwieldy payload out of its nosedive, but the descent continued with alarming velocity towards the waves below. The Fathom swooped at an angle into the tossing waters, lurching back up and vaulting forward, like an oversized wooden pebble skimming across a pond. Twice more it connected with the lashing tide, before finally running out of ocean and carving a sandy scar through the beach that framed the harbor. Trees and dunes gave way to the plunging bow of the Fathom, and a flock of seagulls, hitherto enjoying a civilized game of hopscotch on the shore, scattered like *squawking* pins in a bowling alley.

As the ship screeched and groaned along its freshly furrowed path, Marty covered Kate with a protective arm, shielding her from shredded branches, bouncing coconuts, and startled sea fowl. With a sickening, tearing crash, the Fathom skidded to a shuddering standstill at the cusp of one of the larger sand dunes.

For what seemed like several seconds, and what was indeed several seconds, there was nothing but silence while the chaotic scene dissipated, punctuated by the lapping of the tide against the shore. There was also a hissing sound from above, and from his fetal position at the edge of the deck, Marty squinted up into the rigging. On his perch, Zephyr sat motionless. Steam and smoke issued from his beak and beneath his wings, escaping with a high pitched whistle as though someone had tried to boil too much water in a huge, parrot-shaped kettle.

Next to Marty, Kate untangled herself from a clump of rigging, shaking sand and debris from her hair. Across the deck, a small barrel rolled into an upright position, sprouted feet and scuttled waywardly towards them, pinballing off masts and railings as it approached. Two hefty cloth hands poked out of an open hatch beside the pirouetting barrel, and Oaf hauled himself back up onto the deck. He steadied himself against the large central mast, wiping the dazed expression from his face with a giant paw, before lumbering over to where the barrel had come to rest on its side, tiny feet still poking out from its base and waggling frantically. Oaf grabbed a flapping foot and heaved its owner out of the tiny wooden prison. Whipstaff popped out like a cork from a bottle and landed nimbly on the deck, dusting himself off and patting the tiny giant's broad shoulder gratefully.

Marty picked his way through the wreckage of the Fathom to where the two tiny shipmates stood, still spluttering as the dust and sand settled. "Are you guys all right?"

Whipstaff straightened, wiping dirt from his face and patting his tiny cloth body. "Yep, everything seems to be where I left it."

Oaf glanced down at his lumbering frame before nodding and delivering what appeared to be his favored method of communication. A large, battered paw that rose in a shaky thumbs up. A weak smile followed in support.

Whipstaff was scanning the deck as the Bobs shimmied down from their lofty nests to join the group.

"Where's the captain?" one of the Bobs barked at nobody in particular.

Since nobody in particular answered, Marty spoke up. "Peepers. Mr. Peepers took him." The words rang out like a church bell, and all eyes turned to Marty. He raised a grimy hand to his face, grimacing as the words continued to flow. "He's gone. When the cannonball hit, Peepers just took off, literally. I don't know where he went, but he took Timbers."

Whipstaff kicked the mast he had been leaning against angrily, and next to him, Oaf dropped to his knees, big glistening tears forming impossibly in his button eyes. Marty's words trailed off as Kate appeared at his side, her hand resting on his shoulder. At their side, the two Bobs held each other up, an identically desolate look framing their faces. The crew sat amongst the debris of the Flying Fathom, as lost and broken their stricken vessel.

As Marty searched for words of comfort, or some sort of stirring speech which would galvanize his devastated comrades, he realized his problems were no longer the overriding concern. Since events had given him a reason to step up to the plate, Timbers had been unwavering. Since reality had done ten rounds in a blender, he had been his guide and his friend, and he had done so without question. For the first time in his life, Marty saw his plight for what it was, and realized there were bigger fish to fry. More important battles to fight. And with people relying on him for the first time, even tiny sackcloth, not altogether *real* people, Marty dug deep and found the words he had heard in countless movies but had hitherto never fully comprehended.

Striking the best action hero pose he could muster, he cleared his throat. "Look!" he squealed, rather too highly pitched for his liking, but he had started, and again, all eyes were on him. "We're a man down, well, not a man, erm, a toy I suppose."

"Not a toy!" a voice sprang up anonymously from the group.

"Sorry, sorry, not a toy," Marty added hastily. "Your captain and my friend. I wouldn't have made it this far if it hadn't been for him. I wouldn't have a clue what I was doing here if the truth be told."

Murmurs of approval rose around Marty, and heartened, he pressed on. "Timbers stuck by me when I needed him, and I am not about to stand by when he needs me, when he needs all of us. I know that you won't either!"

The murmurs had turned to fervent growls of agreement. Oaf was holding his hammer over his head and wiping away tears, and the Bobs were jumping up and down feverishly. Marty continued.

"Timbers raised his sword for my cause without hesitation, and I will be damned if I won't raise my sword to his. He wouldn't go down without a fight, and neither will we." Marty was at full speed now and ignored the nagging insistence in his brain that he was just wildly ad-libbing here.

"What we need is a plan. A plan to get our captain back. Who's with me?"

He left the last words of his stirring speech hanging in the air, but they did not hang for long. Whipstaff stepped forward brandishing his blunderbuss. Oaf hefted his weighty mallet onto his shoulder, and wiping a tear from his eye, took a step forward to join his shipmate. The Bobs clearly had no idea how epic speeches worked and simply stood their ground, applauding approvingly. It was good enough.

Casting a glimpse over his shoulder, Marty thought he detected a hint of admiration from Kate as she looked on, smiling slightly and nodding her head. The moment was perfect. They would rescue Timbers, defeat Peepers, and sail off into the sunset. And then reality interjected, even here, where at best it was likely to be laughed and pointed at.

"Erm, that's fine and all," Whipstaff piped up, "but do we know where we're going? Or what we're going to do when we get there?"

The Bobs, silent until now, offered up a double barreled, unified query. "Yes. Where and what?"

Marty raised a finger to interject. Quite where this finger was going to interject to, and with what, he wasn't sure. As had already been made clear, the plan had been to seek out his mirror self and get some answers. His head hurt at the thought of formulating more complex and foolproof heroics. Perhaps it was time to admit he was a one-plan-a-day kind of guy.

At that moment, a muffled voice saved Marty from any further soul searching. "I know where he is," offered the tiny metal disc still clutched in Kate's hand. Since all eyes were currently in the habit of turning to focal points, the compact Kate held suddenly became the center of attention. She opened it, bringing mirror Marty officially into the conversation. "I know where Peepers took Timbers," he imparted smugly.

All eyes moved closer as their owners took several

paces towards the source of the hopeful declaration. "Tell us!" Whipstaff blurted. "Tell us, or I'm stuffing you down Oaf's pants right now." The tiny giant blushed at the sudden threat and hoisted his trousers up firmly.

The miniature mirrored face smiled knowingly. "Why would I tell you? Everything I've done so far, I've done on his orders." The little figure giggled. "This is my neighborhood, too, remember? When you're here I can do what I like and go where I like. He knows that, and we made a deal. He's got a plan and you're all following it, and I'm not going to say any more." He folded his arms defiantly and stuck out his tongue to emphasize the point.

Whipstaff lunged for the compact, just as Kate snapped it firmly shut. She held her hand up to ward off the approaching first mate and spun on her heels. Keeping the hand raised, she calmly strode to the edge of the deck, leaping from it onto the sandy beach a few feet below.

As she disappeared over the side, Whipstaff glanced at Marty, who shrugged and peered over the railings of the ship.

Holding the compact up, apparently so that Marty was still reflected in its mirror, Kate was seemingly engaged in a heated discussion with his mirror counterpart on the beach below. After a few seconds and wild gesticulations she stopped, closed the lid and returned to the side of the ship. Scaling the rigging, she hopped nimbly back onto the deck, offering the tiny metal case to Marty with a wry smile.

Popping the clasp on the compact, Marty again faced his uncooperative reflection, who now peered back sheepishly, the fire and purpose gone from his eyes. "Okay. All right, I'll tell you," he whimpered. "Just keep that one away from me." He nodded at Kate, who was doing her best to look innocent, while unable to stop from looking smug at the same time. Marty pitched an impressed half-smile at her before returning his attention back to his tiny reflection.

Mirror Marty sighed and rubbed his face with his hands. "He will have taken your friend Downtown. They all hang out there, Peepers and his clowns. He wanted you really." He motioned at Marty before continuing. "He just took Captain Fun Size because he knew you'd go after him."

Kate interjected. "Wait, how could you know that?"

Rolling his eyes, Mirror Marty continued. "It's a contingency. Peepers just wants you, Marty." He narrowed his eyes and seemed to step back from the pane of the tiny mirror as though waiting for a response.

Marty looked up from the compact, searching the azure blue sky for something to say. Looking back across the deck at the crew of the Fathom, he was met with expectant eyes, and in them, he found his answer.

Shaking his head, he sighed. "I said we would go after him, and I meant it."

Kate attempted to weigh in with the voice of reason. It was the same voice Marty was trying to ignore in his own head. "You heard him, he's expecting you. It's a trap.

It's actually not even a trap because you know he's waiting for you." She turned to face Marty's reflection with a look of scorn and derision. "We just have to get Marty out of this place. Then it won't matter." The look faded. "Right?" she added, betraying more than a hint of uncertainty.

The face in the mirror snorted a strained chuckle. "That's not how it works. Even if he gets out, this place and everything in it will still be here. And you have no idea the things that Peepers will do to your friend." The end of the sentence tripped out of the compact like a sickeningly gleeful afterthought which made Marty feel nauseous.

Steeling himself, Marty felt the urge to put on the hero hat again, no matter how ill-fitting it felt. "Trap or no trap, we're not leaving him. And besides, since I woke up this morning, he's been my best shot at getting out of this nightmare."

Mirror Marty cast his gaze around the tranquil bay in which the Fathom lay. Waves lapped, the sun blazed, and palm trees wafted enticingly. "Not really a nightmare is it though?" he suggested. "It's quite nice actually."

Marty grimaced. "Whatever. I don't belong here, and I need to get home. Timbers hasn't steered me wrong yet, and I'm not about to leave him hanging ten with the giggle bunch from Hell." Dramatic music swelled inside his head as his heroic speech reached its climax. "We're going for Timbers," he shouted defiantly as cymbals crashed and the brass section surged in his mind.

"Erm…bit far to walk though isn't it?" the compact

pointed out, drawing bum notes and snapped strings from the imaginary stirring soundtrack of Marty's heroism.

Before Marty could reply, Whipstaff cleared his tiny pirate throat behind them. "If I might offer a suggestion. We could use the lifeboat."

Marty turned to face the first mate, his face framed in a 'please explain' expression. Whipstaff was way ahead of him and was already pulling the tarp from a boat-shaped mound at the edge of the deck. Flung aside, it revealed a small boat, maybe ten feet across, but an exact replica of the Fathom. "The lifeboat," Whipstaff declared proudly. "It should still be in working order. I mean, we haven't used it since the great badger invasion."

Off to his left, Oaf winced and shook his head disapprovingly. "So…many…badgers."

Disregarding his shipmate's utterance, Whipstaff hopped into the lifeboat and hoisted three miniature sails. "Are we off, then?"

Marty met Kate's doubtful expression with a shrug and leapt into the boat, beckoning for her to follow. As she embarked, Oaf scrambled clumsily in alongside them, and Whipstaff turned to the remaining crew of the Fathom, still stood amongst the debris of the torn deck. "Bobs!" he announced. "Stay here and get the Fathom ready to set sail, and try and do something about Zeph. He's in worse shape than a three day old lobster."

The Bobs snapped off a salute in stereo and turned their attention to the splintered mast.

Sitting in the lifeboat, Marty felt as though he was a passenger on a children's funfair ride, waiting for it to start. "How do we…set sail exactly?" he enquired to Whipstaff.

The little first mate winked and patted Oaf on the shoulder. The lumbering buccaneer obliged, loping over to the aft of the boat, opening a hatch in the deck. From it, he produced an enormous set of bellows and gave them a practice squeeze. A mighty blast of air, far more than there should have been, sprang forth from the nozzle of the bellows, and Oaf chuckled in approval. He heaved the massive apparatus into the center of the deck and secured it on struts which were fastened in place.

"Right then!" Whipstaff cried. "If we're all aboard, let's be off." With that, Oaf pushed the mighty bellows together, pushing a gargantuan gust of air into the main sail. The tiny boat shuddered, and then lifted off the deck of the Fathom, hanging in the ether for a second before a second gust from Oaf sent them soaring like a kite in a crosswind into the sky.

Gripping the sides of the boat, Marty ventured a look overboard and watched as the deck of the Fathom grew smaller beneath them, the Bobs busily carrying out their repairs to its broken frame. Having finally gotten his 'air legs' (sea legs were obviously redundant on this ship), Marty felt both exhilarated and confused as the lifeboat continued its ascent.

"This shouldn't work. Should it?" He shouted over to Kate over the billowing vents of air from the bellows.

"No," interrupted Whipstaff with a cheeky glint in his eye, "but it does."

Marty was unable to suppress a laugh, borne half from nerves and half from the realization that the nonsense this world continued to present him with continued to catch him off guard. He leaned closer to Kate. "What did you say to him?" he asked. "My reflection. How did you get him to talk?"

Kate smiled as the sky around them shot past at an impossibly increasing rate of knots. Her hair covered her face, but Marty could see she was winking. She tapped her nose with her finger. "Let's find Timbers."

It was dark when Timbers opened his eye. Since it was dark, it didn't help much. Instinctively, he patted himself down, and was dismayed to discover that his trusty cutlass was gone. His trusty hat, however, was still perched trustily on his head. He reached out into the darkness and felt the coarse grain of sack cloth against his fingers. After a few seconds, he realized he was not in fact groping himself and felt around for the neck of the sack. Finding it, Timbers poked out his head, feeling slightly discouraged as he emerged into a slightly less dark room, barely six feet across. Scrambling out of the sack and to his feet, he kicked at the straw, which covered the ground, and scouted his surroundings.

There was a rickety wooden bed in the corner, and a bucket worryingly marked *slop* next to it. "En suite,"

Timbers muttered to himself. "Nice."

On a table next to it perched a tiny lantern that cast a weak, flickering light out into the gloom. Timbers hobbled over and picked it up, casting spooky shadows across the walls as he did so. Unable to contain his boundless enthusiasm for all things fun, and in spite of his predicament, Timbers let out a mock ghostly, "Wooooo," and chuckled to himself. Silence greeted him, and he cleared his throat before setting the lantern back on the table. Above the bed a small, barred window offered no additional light, and was far too high for a tiny pirate to affect an escape.

On the far wall, he spied a small door with a barred window set into it. He snatched up the lantern again and scuttled over to investigate. Craning up to the aperture, Timbers peered out into the darkness beyond, angling the lantern to get a better view. There was nothing to see aside from a stone corridor which spanned off into the blackness to the left and right. On the far wall, however, a hook glinted in the paltry light cast from the lantern. From it hung his cutlass. He gasped and suddenly wished he had massively long arms. Or a key. A key would probably be better.

Timbers traipsed back over to the bed and sat down. He bounced a few times and the wooden struts creaked. "Hmm, not exactly five star," he grumbled.

"I'm sorry it doesn't meet with your approval." The voice slithered through the bars of the door he had only moments ago peered through. It sounded like a rattlesnake being interviewed for the position of a used car salesman, and Timbers jumped back in surprise.

In the dim light of the cell, Timbers could see two frantically bulging eyes peering at him from between the bars of the door. One of the eyes winked and Timbers felt whatever passed for tiny pirate toy bowels loosen. This was not externally evident, however, as the little captain stood and puffed out his chest. "Who's there? Show yourself, ya scurvy dog."

The voice behind the door cackled. "No, if it's all the same to you I think I'll stay here. And I think that, for the time being, you'll stay there, too." Another cackle punctured the stale air. It was a sound that poured into the room like oil spewing from a broken engine. Even though he could not see the owner of those eyes, the perpetrator of that foul emission, Timbers knew this was Mr. Peepers, and he wished more than ever that he had his cutlass at his side.

Peepers continued. "He's coming for you, and when he gets here, you're both going to have ringside seats to the show. And you're never, ever going to leave." The last words were spat with such venom they sounded like steam escaping, and Timbers struggled to compose himself.

"Yeah? Well come in here, and I'll give you something to laugh about. Erm, no, I mean, I'll paint your face a different color. Yeah, that one."

Timbers' more effective follow up put down was lost,

however. The eyes had disappeared from the hole in the door, and only the demonic giggling of the horrendous clown filled the room, slowly receding as Mr. Peepers departed, leaving Timbers to lament his frankly woeful trash talk.

Hunched on the bed, Timbers sighed forlornly. He lay back and wondered how one went about concocting fiendishly clever escape plans.

"Has he gone?"

The voice issued from the window descended hoarsely on Timbers, startling him anew. He jumped up from where he lay, eyeing the barred window suspiciously. "Who's there?" He demanded.

"Listen, just sit tight," the voice commanded, ignoring Timbers' question. "I'm here to get you out."

Timbers brightened. "A jailbreak? Fantastic! I knew you wouldn't leave me high and dry, Marty," he beamed.

The voice from the window replied tonelessly.

"Who's Marty?"

Another billowing plume of air shot into the lifeboat's sails, pushing it upwards through a bank of clouds. They parted as the tiny boat continued its ascent, reaching an apex before diving again. On cue, Oaf heaved the handles of his bellows and blew another mighty blast, taking them out of the descent. Each time momentum was lost, the tiny giant delivered another gust and the lifeboat continued its journey across the heavens, alternating between soaring and plummeting. It was a motion that lacked any kind of discernible grace, but was, in all fairness, propelling them like the proverbial clappers.

Whipstaff gripped the ship's bow, peering over the edge to get a better idea of their progress and location. Occasionally, he would bark directions to his lumbering shipmate, who in turn piped bellowed air into the left or right sails to adjust the course of the vessel. He turned to Marty, who was sat with Kate, the compact lying open in his hands.

"We're past the harbor, we should be there in no time," Whipstaff shouted over the whistle of passing sky.

Marty nodded and returned his attention to the tiny reflection of himself that stared guardedly back at him. "Right, we have some time, so I think you'd better start talking."

Mirror Marty shrugged, "What would you like to talk about? It's nice up here isn't it? Sunshine, sea air, windy pirates." Oaf overheard and blushed.

"Now, now," Kate interrupted. "Remember what we talked about?" Her voice was unerringly calm and bled the smugness from Mirror Marty's tone.

Marty continued. "You know what I want you to talk about. Why does Mr. Peepers want me, where has he taken Timbers, and how do I get out of here?" His question carried an urgency and sharpness he hadn't expected or intended, but it seemed to have the desired effect on his reflection. Either that, or the mysterious threat that Kate had delivered was enough to gain his compliance.

A sigh rose from the tiny compact. "I already told you." A few moments of silence passed, punctuated by an overtly 'Get on with it, then' cough from Kate.

"All right! All right," came the protesting cry from the mirror held in Marty's hands.

"It's like this," Mirror Marty began. "You go to sleep and you have a scary dream. Who is it that invariably pops up to guarantee you wake up in a cold sweat? I guarantee nine times out of ten, people will tell you that it's a big freaky clown. I know you know what I'm talking about. I mean, here we are sitting in your dream and, for the better part of the day, what have you been steadfastly legging it from?" He paused for a moment to allow Marty to absorb the truth of those words.

Marty hated clowns. In that regard, he counted himself in the select, elite group of 'Everybody in the World' since it was universally agreed that clowns spectacularly failed in their one and only purpose in life. Clowns were supposed to make people happy, but they didn't. They made people cry, and shudder, and run away screaming. It was an undeniable fact of life that the thing whose sole purpose is to make us laugh, basically just makes us soil our collective undergarments.

Marty shifted in his seat as the lifeboat lurched into another surging ascent. "So he's just after me because he knows I hate clowns?"

Mirror Marty rolled his eyes. "It's more than that. Peepers exists to scare the bejesus out of you in your dreams. He probably does it to countless others, too, but now he's found someone that is actually awake in their own dream." He waved a hand towards Marty to emphasize his point. "If he's got you, he can do what he does, what he is here to do, and he never has to stop. Instead of receding into the shadows when you wake up, Peepers will have his own captive audience to torment and terrify whenever he wants, for as long as he wants." Further emphasis was not required, but was nonetheless forthcoming. "That's you, buddy."

Marty's head reeled. Unwilling to comprehend the full meaning of those words, it continued to spin and search for a happy place. He felt cold and clammy and just a few short steps away from panic. Before it took hold, however, Marty felt a hand gently grasp his. It was Kate's, pushing back the fear and replacing it with a comforting warmth that steadied the tornado in his mind.

"That's why he took Timbers," Marty murmured, relieved that his voice at least wasn't shaking. "Bait."

Mirror Marty nodded. "Even if you didn't go after him, he would find you eventually. And kidnapping does fall somewhat under his remit anyway, so it was probably an added bonus for him." The tiny reflection sniggered, stopping as he spied the stern and humorless eyes staring down upon him. "Sorry," he mumbled.

Clearing his throat, he continued. "As to where he's taken your little friend, like I said, it's no secret they all hang out Downtown. I'm sure you've seen the signs. If you go snooping around there, don't worry about finding him.

Just look for the scariest place you can find, the chances are he'll be sat in the dark there, waiting for you." The grin was back, perhaps only returning to mock what was quickly turning into a severely unpleasant proposition.

Trying not to think about the dark places he had visited in nightmares past, Marty pressed on with the interrogation. "We'll worry about that when we land. What about how I get out of here?" The shake of the head and shrug that came from the mirror was not the answer Marty was looking for. He flung his hands up in exasperation.

The tiny scream that flew past his ear reminded him he was still holding the compact, and he quickly bought it back down to eye level. Mirror Marty was steadying himself against the sides of the compact frame and shot a frantic glance outward. "Look, I don't know. How would I know? When Peepers was explaining the plan to me, he must have left out the part where I tell you how to escape."

Marty rubbed his forehead. Even if they had a plan, things would not be going according to it at this stage. He felt in over his head, and although the same could be said for most of the events that transpired that day, a course of action was not presenting itself. There was neither a cunning scheme pointing him to, nor a pursuing danger driving him at, a specific direction. Their current purpose seemed only to gallop, head down into the waiting arms of a monster. *At least it was for a noble cause,* he thought.

And hey, if his plan was to arrive without a plan, they might just get in and out before anyone realized what was going on. After all, he himself had very little idea of what was going on, so how could anyone else? Heartened by this thought, Marty set the compact down, stood up, and headed over to where Whipstaff navigated.

Looking over the first mate's shoulder, Marty could see a looming mass of gray buildings, some at the height of the lifeboat, some even higher. And higher still, a static black cloud hovered like a moored airship, shrouding much of what was below in a foreboding darkness. He knelt down next to Whipstaff, craning over the side to get a closer look. "Is that where we're going?"

"That's it; Downtown," Whipstaff replied with unease.

"Looks like a serial killer's vacation spot." The voice from behind Marty was Kate's. She had also come over to admire the frankly depressing view. "Or where colors go to die."

Marty managed a half smile and a reply that was even less comforting. "It might well be. On both counts."

Shifting his gaze from the sprawling mass of monochrome below, Marty upgraded his half smile to an encouraging full one. "It'll be fine. We'll be in and out before anyone even notices."

"In where exactly?" Whipstaff piped up. "We still don't know where the captain is."

Marty flinched. He knew what the next question would be. It would be a request for details of 'the plan.' "Look, we'll ask around. When we get down there, we'll find someone who isn't a clown, and we'll make some enquiries. Then, when we find Timbers, we'll create some sort of distraction, and get him out in the confusion." Marty flinched again, but this flinch was more welcome than the first. That had sounded just like a plan. He had winged it and managed to put a collection of words into the correct order so they sounded like a plan.

"Sounds like a plan," Whipstaff confirmed cheerily, his smile returning, ironically as the boat passed into the ominous shadow of the vast dark zeppelin cloud above them.

Over the sound of rushing wind, Oaf spoke up from his post at the bellows. "Erm, 'scuse me. We're here," he declared, clearly still rationing his words.

Still riding on the crest of the plan he had stumbled into, Marty turned his attention from the view below, issuing an order as he did so. At the exact same moment, Whipstaff made a similar movement and called out. "Take us down," they ordered in unison.

In his enthusiasm to see his plan realized, Marty had completely forgotten he was not in fact the captain of a flying pirate ship, and by proxy was therefore not the captain of this bellows powered lifeboat. He smiled awkwardly at Whipstaff, but the tiny first mate was already holding his hands up. "No, you go on. This is your show," he conceded, smiling. Having observed the behavior for the better part of a day now, Marty delivered the best piratey wink he could manage and re-issued the order to Oaf.

Complying, Oaf stemmed the air from the bellows

and the lifeboat descended steadily, drifting between the tall gray buildings and into the murky streets below. As they made their descent, Marty caught sight of Kate just as she was catching sight of him. Her eyes were a mixture of amusement and admiration, which flushed Marty's face but also provoked a knowing smile from his lips.

"Nice plan," she sang cheekily. "You've even got me believing *you* believe it'll work."

With a new sense of purpose filling him, Marty had convinced himself of his assertions as well. "It'll work." He winked, and it was Kate's turn to blush.

"Like I said," she replied playfully. "I believe you." There was truth in those words, and Marty felt the urge to deliver another cocky wink. So soon after the last one, though, he felt it would come across as some sort of nervous tick, and instead opted for a hasty thumbs up, which he immediately regretted.

Kate giggled. "Are you this sure of yourself when you're not in your own little fantasy world?"

On a roll, Marty replied with a shrug. "I'm always in my own little fantasy world."

She nodded her approval, and Marty remembered again why she had preoccupied his thoughts so much when they first met. The moment between them would have no doubt lasted longer, but before either of them could think up any more flirtatious comments to fence with, a resounding *thud* signaled their arrival back on terra firma.

The landing was textbook, or would have been if

anyone had been demented enough to write a textbook on landing flying boats. Whipstaff wandered up the deck as Oaf busied himself releasing and stowing the huge bellows, which had propelled them on their journey. As they passed, the first mate delivered a nonchalant high five to the massive paw of his compadre. "Nailed that landing. Nice one." He beamed, drawing an even bigger smile of appreciation from his oversized shipmate.

Marty nodded in approval, although secretly he would have quite liked a high five, too. Moving to join Kate at the edge of the deck, they peered out into a grimy, dingy street that stretched out into darkness ahead of them. The pale light from the few working streetlights gave some outline to the surroundings, but were clearly not up to anything more useful than that.

Although the afternoon was in its infancy, it felt like night had fallen under the steady canopy of the storm cloud, and again Kate's hand found Marty's as he moved to disembark from the boat. He glanced back at her, and immediately saw in her face the exact same trepidation that was ringing alarm bells in his own head. "I know. It's not a tourist spot, is it? Let's just do what we have to do and get out of here, okay?"

Kate took a deep breath and nodded, dropping Marty's hand only to swing over the railing and onto the street below. Marty followed close behind and was soon joined by his two pirate cohorts.

As Whipstaff eyed the street, Oaf produced a lantern, lit

it, and held it out to afford a little more light in the gloom.

"I don't like leaving the boat out here," Whipstaff mumbled, wrapping the small protruding anchor chain around a streetlight and securing it with a padlock. "All right people, remember where we parked."

With the lifeboat moored, attentions turned to the street in which they landed. It was desolate, run down, and filthy. A thin mist hung in the air, giving a further chill and forbidding quality to the semi-darkness. Boarded up buildings flanked the road on either side and tattered posters and billboards fluttered eerily, their brand messages having long since been lost to the ravages of time and the elements. Aside from a few figures huddled in doorways, the street was empty, the only movement coming from various articles of debris blowing here and there: tin cans, plastic bags, and even a random beach ball.

Marty hitched up his collar. It had suddenly gotten quite cold as though the wind had picked up. "Come on, this isn't the sort of street we want to be hanging around on for too long."

There were several transient doorway dwellers huddled here and there in the darkness, but a cursory enquiry gleaned nothing but a few death threats and a gibbering proposal of marriage. Marty tried to remain optimistic, however, as there was plenty more street left, and surely one of these slouching troglodytes must know something. He gestured towards the next hunched figure and the group hastened over to where it sat in the entrance to an alleyway. As they approached, the meager glow from Oaf's lantern lit up what appeared to be a huddled vagrant, sitting amongst a bank of small metal cages. He did not stir as they arrived at his side and remained sat on the curb, eyes gazing steadily forward, unblinking. The cages that surrounded him housed ten or twelve brightly colored but miniscule canaries that flapped and skittered about their cages as the party approached.

The vagrant was a bearded man, who looked about three hundred years-old. Dressed in a filthy gray overcoat, tattered black trousers, and grubby worn boots, he sat silent, gargoyle-like, staring straight ahead and seemingly oblivious to his visitors.

Marty cleared his throat in hopes of eliciting a response, which was not forthcoming. "Erm, hello? We're sorry to bother you, but did you happen to see a group of clowns with a small pirate in tow recently?"

Silence greeted the question. The stoic transient's gaze remained fixed on the air six inches in front of him.

"Listen, it's quite important," Marty continued, glancing nervously from side to side. "We need to find our friend. Have you seen him?"

"Why are you asking him?" A new voice boomed out into the gloomy ether, startling everyone but the static hobo. "He doesn't even know what day it is."

Marty's gaze sprang in the direction of the thunderous voice, resting upon the nearest canary that was perched in the closest cage and eyeing them curiously. The tiny bird cocked its head as though studying Marty, and then impossibly spoke again.

"You people are new around here aren't you?" It bellowed in a thick, Jamaican accent. "Are you lost?"

Having recently become somewhat accustomed to having things that really had no business speaking in the first place addressing him, Marty fought back the enquiring prods of reality in his brain and replied, "We're looking for our friend. He was brought here by a group of clowns. Have you seen him?"

The canary ruffled its feathers, bringing a wing up to stroke its tiny chin. "Hmm, there are plenty of clowns around these parts. Don't recall seeing a pirate though. Didier! Have we had any pirates come through here lately?" The last comment was directed at a canary in the adjourning cage, that suddenly stopped pecking at the ground and raised its head in recognition.

"Ah, no, I do not think so," the pecking bird replied with a strong French accent. "All we get through here is clowns, so I would have remembered a pirate." Didier hopped up onto his perch alongside the heavy voiced canary who had addressed him. "Who are these people, Bruno? Do they have any worms?"

The first canary, whose name was apparently Bruno, ignored his friend's question and continued to address Marty, "You'll have to forgive Didier. He is used to the finer things in life. Worms may not seem like much to you, but when all you've got to eat is seed." Bruno made a stab at a shrug, which is no mean feat with only wings to work with. At his side, Didier was still jabbering away in French and attracting the attention of the canaries in neighboring cages.

Sensing this particular line of enquiry was shaping up to be something of a wild canary chase, Marty took a step back. "All right, well, thank you for your time. We'll keep looking." He held his hands out to quell the throng of canary banter welling up from the surrounding cages.

Whipstaff tugged at Marty's jacket. "This is getting us nowhere, let's get going," he chirped, shaking his head.

"No, wait!" a canary with a decidedly German lilt piped up. "This pirate you speak of, is he *winzig?* Is he tiny like you?" it asked, pointing at Whipstaff. "I saw him with the clowns. They came by here not long ago."

All eyes turned to the Aryan aviator. Whipstaff lunged at the cage. "Where did they go?" he shrieked, almost knocking the bird off its perch with his frantic request.

Bruno turned to his winged cellmate. "What are you talking about, Berthold? I didn't see any pirate."

Berthold regained his footing on the perch. "*Ja.* Not long ago." He was addressing Whipstaff now, who had his face pressed against the cage. "These others did not see him, they were looking for worms. Me? I do not care for worms." He shifted awkwardly. "Do you have any cheese?"

Whipstaff turned towards his comrades, away from the bird who was implausibly smiling at the thought of cheese. Oaf checked his pockets redundantly, and Marty shook his head. "No, I'm sorry, we don't have any cheese. Do you know where they went with our friend?"

Berthold deflated slightly, dropping back onto his perch. "I'm sorry, no. You might try the Big Top. It's just up the road. It's where all the clowns go," he imparted sorrowfully, lowering his head and muttering as he did. "No cheese."

Whipstaff was already on the street and scuttling in the direction Berthold had pointed them. Not wishing to lose another pirate, Marty made his farewells brief.

"Thank you for your help," he called over his shoulder as he headed after the fleeing first mate. "I'm sorry we didn't have any worms. Or cheese!" Kate and Oaf were already in pursuit, and in an instant the group was just a dancing lantern glow in the distance.

Bruno flapped his wings at their backs. "Dammit!" he cried. "Sorry guys, no worms." Groans leapt up from the surrounding cages, and Bruno turned to eye the comatose tramp who had remained motionless throughout the proceedings.

"Who are you, anyway?" he grumbled at the motionless figure.

Timbers paced to and fro across the length of his tiny cell, casting impatient glances up at the tiny barred window as he marched. It had been a good ten or fifteen minutes since the mysterious voice from above had promised him freedom, and pirates were not renowned for their patience. Just as he had given up on his erstwhile savior, however, and turned his mind to alternative means of escape, most likely involving some degree of swashbuckling, the voice returned.

"Hey, are you ready to leave?"

Timbers snapped out of his plan making, in which he had dispatched a dozen clowns using only a potato and was making a sharp exit on a giant ostrich. Peering into the gloom, he responded in the affirmative. "Ready when you are, squire."

The words had scarcely left his sack cloth mouth when a resounding boom thunder-clapped through the cell, bringing with it a cloud of dust and debris. Having slightly misjudged his earlier 'Ready' claim, Timbers flew across the cell, buffeted by the blast, and came to rest heavily against the far door. Quickly hopping to his feet, he patted himself down, checking to see if he still had the requisite number of limbs, and then peered into the settling carnage where the window once was. In its place, a hole now opened invitingly, and a green gloved hand beckoned from the other side.

"Come on. It's safe to assume they heard that."

Impressed by the sudden explosion, Timbers scampered to the new exit, chuckling and making satisfied "Boom!" noises. Using the bed as a trampoline, he threw himself towards the protruding hand and grasped it firmly, his momentum carrying him through the breach.

In the darkness of the corridor into which he vaulted,

Timbers could make out a small figure standing before him. Thankfully, it was not clown-shaped, and before the tiny captain could utter another word, it was hightailing in the opposite direction, calling back over its shoulder as it did so.

"Follow me!"

Timbers needed no further encouragement and galloped after his mysterious ally, catching up to him at the end of the corridor. The passageway veered sharply to the right, and Timbers' rescuer was already making good headway in front of him. The light was still annoyingly sparse, and from his vantage point some way behind, Timbers still could not make out who he was following. Given his admittedly limited experience of prison breaks, though, and with his list of alternative options currently at none, he pressed on, attempting to keep up with the silhouetted figure currently bounding away like a grasshopper on steroids. Presently, the corridor terminated at a large metal door, and the figure ahead came to a stop, allowing Timbers to catch up. Pulling up alongside him, Timbers peered upwards, firstly at the door, and then at his liberator.

The former was large and rusted, and not nearly as interesting as the latter. Timbers found himself standing beside a bespectacled old gentleman in a bright green bodysuit. Tufts of gray hair sprouted from beneath a green cowl from which sprang two antennae. Metallic green lycra covered his wiry frame, tapering into tight black leggings which nobody of his apparent advanced years had any business wearing. Transparent gossamer wings ran down his back, and his chest was emblazoned with a shining, silver 'L.'

Catching his breath, the old man glanced down at Timbers and held out his hands reassuringly. "Don't be alarmed. We'll be out of here in a jiffy."

Timbers suppressed a chuckle. "I'm not alarmed, old timer. Confused perhaps." He gestured towards the metal grate. "After you?"

The lycra-suited pensioner turned his attention to the door. "Hmm, an elevator. Invented by Archimedes in 336BC to transport gladiators into the coliseum of ancient Rome." He leaned closer, peering owlishly through his spectacles. "Of course, they were much more rudimentary back then. This one is much more reminiscent of the industrial models employed by Elisha Otis in the 19th century—"

Scratching his head, Timbers interjected, "This is very interesting, it really is, but you didn't break me out for a history lesson. Can we just move this along?"

The old man paused, seemingly surprised at being interrupted mid-lecture, and extended a bony finger to push the button housed on a plate next to the door. A muted bell sounded, followed by the grinding of gears, and finally the door heaved open with a grinding protest to reveal a dank, dimly lit elevator car within.

"Shall we?" The jumpsuited pensioner ushered Timbers inside.

The doors closed behind them, and Timbers' eccentric new friend eyed the row of buttons set against the wall before selecting the highest, marked '1.'

"Going up," he chimed as the elevator grumbled to life around them.

Timbers searched for the words to articulate his confusion. "I take it you're not with the clowns then?" was all he could manage.

"Ah, clowns," The old man declared triumphantly. "Originating in ancient Egypt circa 2400BC; famous examples include Fumagalli, Paggliachi, Cepillin, characterized by Charlie Chaplin, The Marx Brothers, Buster Keaton…"

Timbers loosed an exasperated "Arrrr!" and pounded a tiny fist on the elevator wall. "Yes! Clowns, simple question, you crazy, rum-swiller!"

Stopping mid-sentence, the green suited geezer blinked. "No, no, I'm not a clown." He cast a hand over his costume to display his non-clownishness. "I'm sorry, I do tend to go on a bit sometimes."

Timbers rolled his eyes. This was turning into a high speed taxi ride with a driver who was asleep at the wheel. "I'm sorry," he muttered through his few pirate teeth. "I appreciate the rescue, but who are you?"

The old gent raised a hand to his cowled forehead. "Where are my manners, young fellow?" He turned to face Timbers, hands proudly on hips." I am the Locust."

The little pirate's face melted from irritation to

awe, and he gasped like a star struck fan waiting in line for an autograph. "You're the Locust? My apologies for snapping. I've heard a lot about you!" he gushed, rubbing his hands excitedly.

The Locust nodded and pointed to the silver 'L' which filled his chest.

Timbers continued to enthuse. "I mean, I say I've heard of you. Everyone has, but I don't know anyone who's actually met you. You're something of a mystery. An enigma. I don't even know what you do."

Spreading his arms wide, The Locust affected a suitably impressive crime fighting tone. "Why, this is what I do. I right wrongs, fight injustice, rescue damsels in distress."

Timbers shifted uncomfortably. "Look, I know this is a frock coat, but if you think I'm a damsel, you might want to take those glasses back."

The wizened crime fighter waved his hand dismissively. "Not exclusively damsels. I'll rescue anyone. I just prefer rescuing damsels." He winked awkwardly, and Timbers suddenly felt a little queasy.

"Well, it's still an honor to meet you, sir," Timbers added quickly, eager to not pursue that particular line of enquiry. "What I meant was: why are you called the Locust?"

"Ah, well, I eat books," the Locust replied casually. The words hung in the air for a few moments while Timbers attempted to catch them, put them in the correct order, and try to make some sort of sense out of them.

"You…eat books?" He asked, still wondering if he had

missed some kind of hidden meaning.

The Locust smiled. "Yes. History books, biographies, encyclopedia, fiction, reference, manuals, you name it."

Timbers struggled to comprehend. "But why? It doesn't sound like much of a super power if you ask me."

"Well, no it isn't," the Locust agreed. "But you see, every book I eat goes up here." He tapped the side of his head proudly. "And it's quite useful, you know; knowing everything."

A light bulb illuminated in Timbers' head. "Oh, I see. Yes I suppose that is quite useful. Wouldn't it be easier to just read them, though?"

The Locust blinked thoughtfully. "Oh, heavens no. That would take ages! Besides, they taste quite good."

Before Timbers could unleash a further volley of questions, the elevator came to a jarring stop and its rusted doors groaned open. The sight that presented itself on this floor was decidedly better than the one they had entered the elevator from. Clearly, the decor was aimed more towards splendor and less at prison camp. The floor was carpeted, and the walls draped, holding candlelit sconces at regular intervals. At the door of the elevator, the corridor ended in a T-junction, with two equally splendid hallways spanning in opposite directions. Two bespectacled eyes and one good pirate eye peered out through the open doors, surveying each of the three extruding aisles carefully for signs of movement. Satisfied there was none, the Locust gently motioned to his pint-sized ward that the coast was clear. But before either of them could disembark, a shrill alarm sounded, echoing up through the elevator shaft beneath them.

"Oh, an alarm!" chirped the Locust. "Designed to detect intrusion or unauthorized entry. Invented by Augustus Russell Pope in 1853 and patented by—" he was cut short as Timbers interjected urgently.

"Yes, yes that's fascinating, but hadn't we better be, you know, legging it?"

The jabbering old man nodded in agreement, extending an apologetic hand, which was lost on the already hightailing Timbers. As they bolted from the elevator into the corridor opposite, a flurry of activity emanated from the flanking passageways. Neither Timbers nor his newfound crime fighting ally had any desire to discover the source of the activity as they made their escape. And yet, as the commotion behind them grew louder, the little captain could hear heavy flapping footfalls of the sort that might be caused by oversized shoes. As they grew louder still, almost gaining, Timbers thought he could make out another sound.

He thought he heard giggling.

Marty rounded the corner at the end of the street and almost fell over Whipstaff, who had stopped in his tracks and stared up at the building that monopolized the skyline in front of them. The vast structure stretched epically skywards and would have cast a mighty shadow upon them, had any sunlight been able to penetrate the foggy gloom of the city.

It seemed to be made up entirely of lights, which starkly contrasted the gray, miserable mood of the street below. Some moved on giant wheels, some adorned giant balloons, and some surrounded the gigantic sign that proudly announced 'The Big Top Club' to all those who hadn't already caught on to the overall vibe of the place. In keeping with the theme, the whole façade of the building gave the impression of a huge marquee tent, although closer inspection revealed what appeared to be canvas was, in fact, brick and masonry.

Illuminated by the dancing, animated spectacle, Marty and Whipstaff stood hypnotized as Kate and Oaf rounded the corner and clattered into them, the lantern almost lost in the pile up. It was scarcely enough to drag their attention away from what lay before them.

Even as Oaf stooped to retrieve the fallen lantern, he gazed upwards, mouth open in awe and surprise. "Ohhh, pretty lights," was all he could muster in the face of this multi-colored extravaganza, however.

Moving towards it inexorably, like penguins to a fishmonger, the group advanced slowly. As they did, three figures hastened across the street in front of them and climbed the flight of steps to the door of the Big Top. As they flung open the doors, muffled sounds of music could be heard from within, receding back into obscurity as the doors closed behind them.

Marty turned to his companions. "They didn't look like clowns. We might actually be able to pull this off." Aware that all eyes were on him, he continued. "I mean, this should be a lot easier than we thought."

Rather than wait for any possible questions or protests, he crossed the street and vaulted the few steps to the front doors. Atop the flight of stairs, Marty turned to beckon his friends, but momentum, or perhaps curiosity, had carried them to his side already. *Or maybe they just believed him,* he thought, smiling to himself. Never having been a leader before, he was unsure which was more likely, but was buoyed by the solidarity nonetheless. Taking a deep breath, he grasped the handles of the huge double doors.

"Is everybody ready?" he asked, expecting a resounding affirmative. Looking down, Marty caught sight of Whipstaff hefting the blunderbuss off his back, and wielding it menacingly. "Hey," he whispered hoarsely. "Put that away. We're not resorting to 'All Guns Blazing' yet."

The little first mate grudgingly obliged. From the rear of the party, Oaf let out a short, "Oh! Erm," and everyone turned. The tiny giant raised the lantern, opened its tiny window and blew out the candle within. Clearly sensing he was holding up proceedings, he hooked the lantern to his belt and smiled sheepishly. "Sorry, ready now."

As he reached out to grasp the large brass door handle, Marty was halted by a hand tugging at his jacket. He turned to meet Whipstaff's cautious gaze, an equally cautionary sack cloth finger wagging in front of it. "Stay your blade, matey. We can't just go swanning in there like this. Peepers is expecting you, right? You need a disguise."

Marty tutted. Whipstaff was right, and while a bucket of face paint and a hilariously fluffy wig might have been just the ticket, he hadn't exactly packed for this trip.

"Hey, maybe the old guy with the birds will lend you his coat," Kate suggested.

Marty shook his head. "No, I don't think they'd let us in if I looked like a zombie scarecrow with a hangover. Besides, from the smell of him, I wouldn't be surprised if that coat was actually a part of him."

The group nodded solemnly, almost as one, and Marty was relieved they had seen his point of view. He was on board with the disguise idea, but not with the notion that the disguise might give him rabies.

Whipstaff snapped his fingers, bringing Marty back to the job at hand. Reaching up, the little first mate untied his bandana and handed it to Marty proudly. Reaching to retrieve it, Marty froze, suddenly unable to take his eyes off the enormous afro which had just been freed and was sitting grandly atop Whipstaff's head. Kate was doing her best not to stare, while Oaf simply raised a cloth paw to his mouth, holding back a broad, throaty chuckle.

Whipstaff rolled his eyes and sighed, shaking the bandana impatiently. "Just take it. It's the sea air, it makes my hair so unmanageable," he muttered.

Joining his companions in wholly failing to mask his amusement, Marty took the bandana and tied it around his face, so that only the top half was now visible. It would do.

"Haha!" Whipstaff chirped. "It fits well, *señor*, now all you need is a *sombrero*."

Marty grinned behind the bandana, in no small part because he was now picturing himself as a Mexican bandito." Yeah, ok Captain Seventies. Let's go." Turning back to the entrance of the Big Top, he pushed the doors, following them as they swung inwards. Following on behind, the group came to an unruly rest against a small, raised balcony rail. The sight which met them was even more resplendent than anything the towering building's impressive exterior had to offer.

Spanning out in front of them was a cavernous chamber, brightly lit and even more brightly colored. Marty's little band stood on a raised walkway, which ran around the edge of the room, dipping in places to allow access to the intricately mosaicked central floor depicting a leering clown's face. To say that this was a dance floor, however, would be somewhat inaccurate. There were figures dancing on it, a large group in fact, but they seemed suspended, hovering in midair, swooping and whirling impossibly just above the ground. Although the floating dancers were not especially clownish in appearance, they all wore gaudy masquerade masks that afforded them an exaggeratedly grotesque aspect nonetheless.

Bordering the dance floor was an implausibly long bar propped up by surly patrons, each paying more attention to their drinks than to the band churning out the disjointed carnival music from the stage opposite. At the hub of the stage, a five piece were set up, plucking, beating and blowing a discordant melody out into the crowd.

While nobody turned to witness their arrival, Marty was acutely aware the arrival of two pirates and a Mexican bandit would surely spark some interest sooner or later and quietly waved for his companions to follow him. A clutch of unassuming, out of the way, booths beckoned, and Marty led the way across the raised gantry to where the music was more muted and the light less incriminating.

"Right," piped up Whipstaff. "What now?"

Marty eyed the bar and its clientele dubiously, hoping to spy a friendly face. Most of them either scowled back or mooched vacantly over their drinks. None appeared to be candidates for a quick game of twenty questions. "Erm, I'm not sure. Shall we get a drink?" he suggested eventually.

Whipstaff frowned and reached up to the handle of his blunderbuss again. He had likely been expecting to have committed a lot more violence and doing way less drinking, but as both appeared right up there with his other favorite pirate things to do, he relaxed his grip on the weapon and called over a waiter. A steward duly obliged, scuttling over with a tray.

He was dressed in billowing satin pantaloons and enough greasepaint to redecorate the inside of the Big Top Club, and yet he did not have the look of a clown about him. *Perhaps he was a clown in training,* Marty thought, chuckling to himself. On probation until he'd learned how to juggle and scare small children.

Whipstaff wasted no time with the order. "Four of everything, please," he commanded. "And whatever my friends want."

Marty waved the attendant away, clearly remembering the tequila ambush and subsequent conflict with the beer monkeys that very morning. Besides, keeping a clear head when riding the runaway mine cart that was his plan was probably a good idea, he decided. Kate had evidently made a similar decision, shaking her head as the waiter turned to her.

As he left with Whipstaff's order, Oaf belatedly spoke up. "I will have…" he began before looking up and realizing he was talking to no one. He sank back into his seat, mumbling. "I only wanted water."

Kate leaned towards Marty, speaking in barely a whisper. "So, what do you think? Does anyone here look approachable?"

"Do any of them look capable of speaking at all?" Whipstaff interjected.

Cautiously removing the bandana covering his face, Marty scanned the crowd. None of them looked like the kind of person who would apply the brake if they were speeding towards him in a steamroller let alone consent to engaging in some form of conversation. His eyes met those of a tall, willowy barmaid who smiled at him suggestively. She lacked the homicidal air of the surrounding drinkers, and Marty managed a nervous smile in return.

"She'll do," he imparted absently. Whipstaff followed his gaze.

"Damn right she will!" he cheered in agreement, jabbing Oaf with a hearty elbow.

Oaf chuckled timidly, scratching his head as he did so, obviously not sure of what his shipmate was alluding to but happy to be involved.

Suddenly remembering Kate was next to him, Marty turned to face her. "I mean, she'll be a good person to ask. She's a barmaid, people talk to her. And she looks friendly." He tried to make the last part sound innocent, a feat clearly not helped by further giggling and elbow jabbing from Whipstaff. Oaf at least was not laughing anymore. His confused expression confirmed he did indeed have no idea what was going on, and didn't really like being elbowed repeatedly.

Turning back towards the bar, Marty watched as the barmaid stopped a waiter carrying drinks, relieved him of his cargo, and headed towards their table. Her eyes remained fixed on Marty's as she slinked across the room, effortlessly slaloming to and fro to avoid patrons as she approached. As she arrived at the booth and placed the tray of drinks gently onto the table, Marty tried valiantly not to gawp. Dressed in lavish, sparkling satin, the barmaid looked more like she belonged on a catwalk than in a funhouse, and from the look on her face, she knew it.

Whipstaff ceased his giggling, and he and Oaf fidgeted bashfully in their seats as Marty searched for some kind of greeting to cut the silence.

"Welcome to the Big Top. You're new here, aren't you?" Her voice was so Eastern European that umlauts seemed to hang in the air over the table as she spoke, and while she was clearly talking to the whole party, her eyes remained firmly fixed on Marty. "My name is Ursula. I run the bar here. Anything you need, you come to me." Again, she grinned at Marty, who was fast running out of other places to look. Deciding instead to be bold, and in spite of his earlier pledge of abstinence, he snatched up a shot glass from the tray and dispatched its contents defiantly. The ghost of the morning's hangover briefly stirred to remind Marty of what he had consumed for breakfast before mercifully retreating again, allowing Marty to continue with his bravado induced display.

"We're looking for our friend." He began firmly, and perhaps a little too loudly, as a few patrons looked up from their drinks. "We were told he came this way recently. With some…clowns," he added in a tone he hoped was less conspicuous.

Ursula the bar maid raised an eyebrow. "We don't get clowns in here very often," she crooned. "They keep to themselves when they're not out giving someone nightmares."

Marty looked up, scanning the room and its garishly attired clientele.

Clearly having had the same thought as he was having, Kate interjected. "The people here though, the staff, the building. If it was anymore clowny in here, you'd be handing out free balloons at the door."

Oaf craned his neck hopefully back to where they had entered, but alas, no balloon vendor was present.

Ursula waved a faintly derisory hand at Kate. "We keep up the appearance, yes. They seem to leave us alone, and of course carnival chic is very in at the moment."

Oaf and Whipstaff nodded absently, although for all they knew, flying gerbil chic could have been in at the moment.

"As to whether I've seen your friend, what does he look like? Is he as handsome as you?" Ursula purred, cocking a playful glance and another raised eyebrow at Marty.

Again, robbed of words by those sultry eyes, Marty was relieved Kate still had a couple left.

"No. He's a pirate. Like these two," she muttered, gesturing to Whipstaff and Oaf, who had lost all interest in the conversation and were busy throwing beermats at each other.

"A pirate you say?" Ursula pursed her lips. "We see even fewer of them here." She paused, squinting into the distance behind them. "Does he wear a big blue coat?"

Marty blinked in surprise. "Yes. Yes he does."

Whipstaff and Oaf called a truce to their beermat battle and peered over at the waitress expectantly.

"Does he wear a hat? And an eye patch?" she continued.

Nodding, Kate attempted to hurry things along. "That sounds like him. Have you seen him?"

Still staring out over the dance floor, Ursula raised an elegant hand and extended an immaculately manicured finger towards the stage beyond. "I have. Right over there."

As one, the group craned in the direction of the pointing finger. On the stage beyond the dance floor, behind the manically caterwauling band, Timbers scuttled out from behind a curtain. Momentarily caught in a spotlight, he paused, glancing out into crowded room. Before Marty had the chance to call out to his tiny companion, a little old man dressed in green lycra leaped out from behind the same curtain, scampering past Timbers and motioning for the little pirate to follow.

Whipstaff and Oaf were already on their feet, vaulting onto the table and sending bottles and glasses skittering to the floor. "Captain!" Whipstaff bellowed as he sprang off the table and made for the dance floor, Oaf close at his heels. Clearly the music had drowned him out as Timbers took off across the stage after the leotard clad geriatric.

Marty rose to follow his shipmates, and turned briefly back to address Ursula as he did so. "Sorry about all this. Thank you for you hospita–" His sentence was cut short as Kate grabbed his hand and launched them both after Whipstaff and Oaf into the throng of the dance floor.

The two brigands were already carving a path through the dancing horde. Oaf's huge wooden mallet spun and scythed, knocking patrons hither and thither as they made for the stage. In an act of politeness belying his appearance and chosen profession, Oaf galloped apologetically through the crowd.

"Excuse me. Sorry. Pardon me. I'll pay for that. Get some ice on that," he shouted as he swung his hammer, literally beating a path to the stage and his captain.

Behind him, Whipstaff was riding the slipstream created by his lumbering shipmate and was eyeing the stage for signs of Timbers. The little captain and his mysterious aged cohort had vanished behind the curtain at the far side of the stage. Marty had seen it, too, as he and Kate hurried on behind. They were close to the stage now and could see a door behind the far curtain. This must surely have been Timbers' escape route, and he hoped that the dervish that was Oaf, at the head of the carnage being perpetrated on the dance floor, had seen it also.

It appeared he had. He reached the stage at the same velocity as a ballistic missile and leapt onto it mid-hammer swing.

Incredulously, the band continued to play as first Oaf and Whipstaff, and then Kate and Marty arrived on stage, tearing past them to where Timbers had exited stage left. The door had already been flung open when Marty and Kate reached it. Whipstaff and Oaf vanished into the blackness beyond, clearly desperate to be reunited with their captain. Resting a hand on the door frame, Marty glanced back into the Big Top. Everything was as it had been before their manic trip across the dance floor. Patrons sipped their drinks, dancers whirled about, and waiters pirouetted through the crowd with their laden trays. Only Ursula remained where she had been, staring out across the dance floor from their now deserted booth. She flashed a Hollywood smile and shot Marty a heavy eyelashed wink, nodding knowingly as she did so. She was not part of this facade. She knew it, and now he knew it, too. He nodded his brief thanks before Kate's hand, which was still firmly grasping his, yanked him purposefully into the shadows beyond the stage door.

As Marty disappeared through the open doorway, a gang of gibbering clowns entered stage right. Like bloodhounds on a scent, they charged over to where the group had made their escape, and tilted headlong, almost as one, through the door into the darkness beyond.

Had Marty and Kate been aware of the psychotic pursuers snapping at their heels, they may have moved quicker as they arrived in the gloom that was backstage. Thanks largely to a steep flight of stairs this decision was made for them. Gravity roughly assisted them into a large and equally dingy chamber. Coming to an ungainly stop at the foot of the stairs, Marty squinted into the vaguely lit room. There was no sign of any of the crew of the Fathom or the aged stranger who had been accompanying Timbers. Rising to his feet, Marty surveyed his surroundings while helping Kate regain her footing.

There was scarcely enough time to take in the stark, emptiness of what was essentially a huge, connecting corridor when the sound of several giggling maniacs invaded the blackness at the top of the stairs.

Branching out from where they stood, there were half a dozen corridors offering a possible means of escape. Marty wasted no time in choosing the nearest, grabbing Kate by the hand and steadfastly legging it away from the nightmarish sounds of mayhem from above.

Luckily, the sounds of pursuit seemed to diminish as they ran. "They're not following," Marty gasped, wishing he was fitter. "Maybe they don't do so well on stairs with those big, flappy feet."

Kate seemed to be a little less out of breath and a lot less optimistic. "Yeah, or maybe they know their way around down here."

Running as they were through a dark, nightmarish corridor underneath a nightclub decked out like a big top circus tent in a city full of clowns, it was hard to not concede she might have a point. *That was no reason to stop, though,* Marty thought. The last evidence of pursuit was behind them and, therefore, the logical course of action must surely be to swiftly bolt in the opposite direction. The corridor presently opened into another large, elongated room full of boxes and crates. Indeed, the whole complex network of tunnels and chambers underneath the Big Top appeared to be just an oversized storage area.

Marty and Kate stopped in the entrance to this new room, scanning for signs of their pirate comrades. Nothing stirred, save for the sound of their own breath, echoing slightly in the dank silence of the hall. It seemed this chamber was as elaborately interconnected as the one they had recently vacated, and Marty realized it would be very easy to get lost in a place like this. Skirting the wall slowly, the pair edged towards the nearest connecting passageway, avoiding the debris that cluttered the floor.

The silence was only broken as Kate nudged a section of broken packing crate, sending its unhinged lid clattering loudly to the floor. For a moment, everything stopped. Marty froze in his tracks, his breath held for what seemed like minutes. From the darkness behind them, and far too close for comfort, a throaty chuckle rose up, slowly becoming more frantic and high pitched. The breath that had been held flew sharply as Marty dove behind the nearest large crate, pulling Kate into the shadows behind him. The giggling seemed to get louder and louder before abruptly stopping, seemingly only a few feet from where they hid.

There are very few things in life that have the capacity to paralyze a person with fear. It could have been the situation he currently found himself in, but Marty could only think of one. As he turned to peer through the slats of the crate he crouched behind, his mind was full of leering, gleeful grins, shrill cackling laughter, and brightly colored psychopaths with ghostly white faces. Fearing just such a sight, Marty surveyed what he could see of the room beyond. Nothing sneered back at him out of the blackness. The room itself seemed to be waiting for a reaction, silent and pensive.

Glancing over his shoulder, Marty motioned to Kate that they needed to keep moving. Despite the graveyard serenity of their surroundings, something was there, and if not, it soon would be. It was then that the something that may or may not have been there declared its presence. Slinking out of the darkness on the other side of the crates, a brightly dressed, but hideously painted, harlequin surveyed the room with soulless, bulging eyes. Even within the gloom, and from his restricted vantage point, Marty could tell it was Mr. Peepers.

His eyes burned balefully, and a thick guttural chuckle issued from between his upsettingly crooked and jaggedly sharp teeth. Shrinking back behind the crates, Marty felt sure he would be spotted. Although undercover, he could still feel those blazing pupils scanning for him as he crouched in the darkness.

"So, it's a game of hide and seek is it, sonny?" The voice spilled out of the blackness like hot molten evil, and Marty gasped much louder than he would have liked. "I must warn you. I am very good at hide and seek," the voice continued, leering out of the shadows, seeking him out.

As Marty edged away from his ghastly pursuer, the voice spoke again, seemingly all around them as it bounced off the cold stone walls. "Why don't you come out? We only want to play. We only want you to stay here with us. Imagine the fun we can have." The last sentence again trailed off into a growling, sneering chuckle, filling Marty's imagination with all sorts of things, none of them remotely fun.

As they made their way cautiously past a stack of scrap wood leaning against the wall, Marty's foot scraped the floor, and Kate winced as the sound rasped through the chamber. It was immediately met by a hoarse squeal of demonic delight, and suddenly the voice seemed to shriek from behind them.

"Come out!" Again it chanted feverishly, "Come out! Come out!"

The third time it was almost alongside them and singing with cheerful ferocity. "I…Will…Find…You…!"

Something in Peepers' voice seemed to catch Marty by the throat, squeezing icy talons that left him breathless and frantic. It drifted formlessly, threatening to seek them out without the need for glaring eyes or grasping hands. As terrifying as Mr. Peepers was to look at, hearing that voice getting closer and closer, creeping like a ghostly fog, was the real stuff of nightmares. Pulling together all his courage, Marty ventured another peek over the top of the crates behind which they cowered. Mr. Peepers stood a few feet away on the other side, mercifully with his back to them. Recoiling, Marty could still make out Peepers as the clown sloped jerkily away to the other side of the room, where he disappeared into the far corridor.

Feeling able to breathe again, Marty grasped Kate's hand firmly in his and made his way across the wall of the dimly lit chamber. The nearest connecting corridor was only a few feet away and yet with every step he expected to hear footfalls behind, or feel a heavy, white-gloved hand on his shoulder. Mercifully, they arrived at the corridor unmolested, sneaking out of the shadows and into the relative safety of the passageway. As they vacated the room, they glanced over their shoulders one last time.

Standing motionless, only a few feet away was a smile on legs. The grinning freak had not been there seconds ago as they had made their escape, yet stood there now, rakish and gaunt, glaring with wild bulging eyes. It was not Mr. Peepers but, instead one of his gleeful cohorts, and it was no less horrifying. Before Kate could scream, the motionless harlequin barked out a violent, piercing laugh, opening its mouth impossibly wide, and displayed wickedly sharp teeth within.

Kate was frozen to the spot as grasping, gnarled white claws reached for her. Claws that would have caught her had Marty not hauled her into the corridor ahead. The clown snatched at thin air, shrieking, and Kate flew backwards into the darkness, clearly thankful to still be holding Marty's hand.

Marty, feeling very much like the dashing hero at this point, sped into the dimly lit passageway, only to crash headlong into a figure lurking within. Skittering to the ground, Marty instinctively raised his fists, expecting imminent unpleasantness. Whirling upon his opponent, Marty mustered the best battle cry he could muster, which tailed off shakily as the assailant stepped into the light. Whipstaff, clearly mystified by the surprise collision, held out his hands defensively. "Whoa, whoa, whoa! It's me, stand down sailor."

Marty dropped his hands, clearly relieved to see the first mate. "Whipstaff. We've been looking for you guys. Where have you been?"

"We've been looking for the captain. This place is like a labyrinth."

"Well, we need to get moving, there's a clown right behind us," whispered Marty. To illustrate the point, two beady eyes hoved into view at their backs, glinting in the shadows. A wide, toothy grin joined them, followed by their owner, towering over Marty, Kate, and Whipstaff while cackling balefully.

"Is that him?" Whipstaff enquired.

Marty sighed, turning incredulously towards the tiny pirate. "Yes, Whipstaff, I believe that's him."

The clown stepped forward out of the darkness, its raised hands causing sinewy shadows to dance across the walls. Standing at full height now, the clown glared at them with burning, murderous eyes that seemed to glow and bulge ever wider. Retreating slowly backwards, Marty briefly considered turning tail and running. This plan, of course, meant turning away from this monster before them, something that would require more courage than he could muster at this moment. Still, the clown crept closer, leaning over and chuckling with demented intent. As it stooped to commit all manner of unspeakable acts upon the shrinking trio, a large, round shape dropped out of a hole in the ceiling overhead.

With a resounding thud, the shape crashed into the

clown, sending both circus freak and mystery arrival sprawling in a heap on the floor.

Marty craned forward, trying to see what had dispatched their attacker. In the dim light of the passageway, Oaf peered up from his perch atop the felled clown. Recognizing Marty, he shot a broad grin and waved cheerfully. "Hello!"

Whipstaff was immediately at Marty's side. "Oaf! Where in Poseidon's paddling pool did you come from?"

"Erm. Up there." Oaf shrugged, pointing vaguely at the large vent in the ceiling.

Whipstaff laughed, springing forward and slapping Oaf briskly on the back. "Well, good timing, me hearty!" He turned towards Marty. "See? I told you this place was like a maze. We better find the captain and get out of here before any more of these jokers show up."

"No argument there, but which way?" Kate enquired. "We can't go back the way we came."

Whipstaff beckoned for them to follow. "Don't worry, I think there's a way out this way. I only doubled back because I heard your voices." He was walking back the way he had come and beamed cheekily over his shoulder. "Lucky for you I did, or you might have been in trouble here."

As Oaf followed on behind his first mate, Marty patted the lumbering pirate softly on the back. "Lucky for you more like. Nice going, big guy." The blushing nod Oaf returned was not seen in the gloom of the basement, but Marty knew it was there, nonetheless.

Creeping to the end of the corridor, Marty caught up to Whipstaff, who seemed to have a much better idea of where he was going. "Have you seen Timbers down here?" he asked.

Whipstaff reached the end of the passageway and paused, looking up and down the connecting corridor, but not back at Marty. "No. He's got to be here somewhere, though."

Kate arrived at the junction and stooped to address Whipstaff. "Look, if he's down here, he'll be looking for a way out, too. We need to do the same thing. Looking for Timbers will be a hell of a lot easier away from where we don't have to worry about being juggled to death."

In the faint glow cast by a flickering light bulb overhead, Whipstaff shook his head defiantly, an imploring look on his face. Marty found himself shaking his head in unison. As much as he spectacularly didn't want to be in the situation they were in at that moment, and as much as his instinct screamed at him to bolt for the nearest exit, they had come for Timbers, and they were going to leave with Timbers.

"We're not going anywhere without the captain," a voice exclaimed. Marty was both surprised and heartened to discover it had come from him.

Kate rose to face him, clearly afraid but hiding it beautifully. "Okay, you're the boss." She turned to Whipstaff. "So, which way?"

Completely ignoring the question, the tiny first mate peered into the darkness behind them. Following his gaze,

Marty squinted back down the corridor they just traversed. Four sets of eyes stared back at them and seemed to be approaching with alarming speed. The group backed away instinctively.

"Which way?" Kate asked again, much more urgently than the last time.

Whipstaff pointed at the approaching harlequins as he prepared to wholeheartedly leg it along the connecting corridor. "Not that way!" he shrieked as he took off at speed.

Clearly not needing an invitation to follow, Marty, Kate, and Oaf took off after him, the sound of chasing, chuckling sideshow freaks behind them. After only a few galloping steps, however, the corridor came to a debris strewn dead end. Scanning the walls feverishly, Marty spied a grubby looking hole, which looked like it could, at some point, have been a laundry chute. With the sound of whooping and screeching maniacs mere moments behind them, it was the only available choice.

Hoisting Whipstaff up to the hole, Marty barked out orders to his fleeing cohorts. "Quickly, down the laundry chute."

"I'm not jumping in that!" Whipstaff protested. He struggled as Marty stuffed him head first into the aperture. "It smells horrible down there."

"Look, just get in. I don't care if it smells funny."

As they dove into the opening, Marty realized he had seen this in a movie at some point, and as he recalled, it had not ended well. With no other option at hand though, he took a deep breath and launched himself, screaming into the blackness of the chute.

There is no good way to land in a heap. Even if you land on top of the heap, there's elbows and other sharp objects to consider. The whole heap landing process is completely without redeeming factors.

These thoughts filed aimlessly through Marty's mind as he landed in said heap atop his flailing comrades at the bottom of the laundry chute.

The room into which they had plummeted was decidedly larger and significantly brighter than the dingy labyrinth they had negotiated moments before. It appeared to be an oversized, underground car park, housing vehicles of every conceivable type, stretching back further than Marty could see. Already on his feet and helping up the others, he could still here the giggling pursuit issuing from the tunnel above them and was already looking for the exit. No immediate means of escape was evident, so without hesitating, Marty sprang over to the nearest car, jiggling the handle frantically. Following his lead, Kate took the next one, but also found it locked. Glancing back at his two pirate allies, Marty had time to see the 'What the hell are you doing?' look on Whipstaff's face, and the 'Is this a game? Can I play?' expression from Oaf, before their four ghoulish pursuers slid out of the tunnel behind them. Even before Marty could switch his attention to the looming monsters, the grunt and growl of a thunderous engine roared into life from the rows of vehicles off to their right.

Whirling round to discover the source of this new sound, Marty's eyes widened as a glittering array of steel and chrome squealed out from amongst a row of parked cars. Swerving violently, it gunned forward, a blur of bright red and silver. Time slowed again, to such a degree that Marty had time to ponder on the fact that he really should be getting used to this time slowing down lark by now, before the screeching tornado of metal tore past him, Kate, and the pirates. Wheeling to track its progress, he watched open-mouthed as the jolting, tilting behemoth clattered into the four gibbering clowns, sending them looping into the air like brightly colored crash test dummies.

Performing a delicate, yet ear-shattering hand brake turn, the silver and red dervish came to a smoking, hissing stop in front of Marty and his friends.

With time now back to normal again, they stood in awe of their shining savior. Towering over them, glittering in the neon overhead lights, engine still grumbling heavily, was a polished red and silver ice cream van. Sitting proudly on its roof was a huge ice cream cone that spouted flowing plastic ice cream scoops. From its open side window, a beaming pirate leaned out, holding a smaller version in his cloth hand. "Any of you land lubbers want one with sprinkles?"

"Timbers!" they cried as one, all taking several steps towards the now stationary van.

"Steady on now, one at a time. Correct change only please," Timbers mocked, before glancing over at the recently felled clowns. Spying movement, his tone darkened. "Second thought, everybody in and let's get our ices out of here." The stern tone had, as always, not lasted long. "Do you see what I did there? Ices, because of the van and, you know…" He chuckled.

Marty clambered into the back of the van. "Timbers, it's fantastic to see you, but can we please just get out of here?" he requested as calmly as he was able. Timbers suppressed further chuckles and rapped sharply on the divider between them and the cabin. The van lurched into life, sending Marty and his companions into an impromptu seated position on the floor of the now speeding vehicle.

There was more that Marty wanted to ask, like where Timbers had been, and how he had escaped, but Kate was already making a more pressing enquiry. "Erm, if we're all in here, who's driving?"

Sliding the partition to the cabin to one side, Timbers gestured for them to take a look. "My friends, allow me to introduce you to the Locust." He dragged a sweeping arm in a pointing motion to the front of the van. Sitting, jaw firmly set in an expression of concentration, and peering owlishly over the steering wheel, was a lycra-clad, little old man. Glancing up from his seat, the Locust smiled amiably and nodded in acknowledgement.

Marty frowned, aiming a question at the old timer behind the wheel. "Where did you get the keys to this thing? And why an ice cream van?"

Even as the query left his lips, Timbers was raising a hand to his face. "No! Don't ask him anything," he cried, but it was too late.

"Well, young man, I hotwired the vehicle you see? It's simply a case of connecting the two wires, which complete the circuit, turning on the fuel pump and all necessary components. That is of course, unless the vehicle is an older model and has a single ignition coil and distributor, in which case…"

Pushing them all back into the rear of the van, Timbers cut the Locust off mid-sentence, although he continued to ramble on to himself as the little captain closed the partition again. "He's a bit of a talker. Best not to ask him anything because you'll get the full, unabridged answer." Timbers sighed, before moving on to Marty's second question. "And why an ice cream van? Why not?" He exclaimed, clapping his hands delightedly. "You can't tell me you've never wanted to make a daring high speed escape from a gang of clowns in an ice cream van. I think we all have, right?"

Marty was about to reply when he realized that, when you look at it like that, it really was hard to disagree.

From the cabin, a muffled elderly voice butted in. "Pardon me, there seems to be an obstruction up ahead. Thoughts, anyone?"

Marty hauled the partition open again, peering out of the windscreen as he sat down next to the Locust. The van was speeding past lines of stationary vehicles towards what appeared to be the car park's exit. Spanning the exit, and blocking their path, was a long wooden tollgate complete with blinking red lights and an imposing looking 'Stop' sign. From the connecting booth, two leering clown faces lit up as the van's headlights flashed in through its window. Even from this distance, Marty could see them skitter out to the gate in front of them, growing bigger and more threatening as the van roared ever forward.

Snapping Marty back from the hypnotic impending collision ahead, the Locust reiterated his enquiry. "Are we continuing forward or should we seek an alternative escape route?"

Marty had seen this hundreds of times in movies. How hard could it be? Quickly buckling his seatbelt, he shot a glance at the rallying pensioner beside him. "Floor it!" he barked, bracing himself against the dashboard. "We're going through."

The van compliantly lurched forward, appearing to bellow a mechanical war cry as the pedal was introduced firmly to the metal. The exit, with its two freakish car park clowns, was barely fifty feet away as Marty squinted out through the windscreen. The van seemed to be going at light speed as they reached the tollgate, main beams glaring and engine screaming. Both red nosed guards dove aside as the gate shattered like kindling, spewing splinters of wood and glass out into the street beyond. The van jolted and slewed crazily through the wreckage, snaking out into the road and lurching heavily to the right. Marty fought to hold his composure, and his lunch, as he shot the Locust a disbelieving look. Whoever this old geezer was, he sure could drive. Several thudding impacts shook the side of the van, and Marty craned to look behind him just as Timbers leapt into the cabin.

"We're out. I think it's time to punch it," he crowed triumphantly, reaching over to the dashboard and flicking a switch next to the radio. Immediately, a jolly, electronic melody sprang from the giant cone above them, as the van's tires caught purchase on the tarmac and sent them zooming away.

Marty unbuckled his belt and made his way shakily into the back as they continued their escape. Whipstaff was peering out the side window, back the way they had come. "Something hit us?" Marty enquired, asking about the thumps as the little first mate pulled his head back in through the window.

Grimacing, Whipstaff nodded. "Aye. Pies. They were throwing custard pies at us, the scurvy dogs."

Oaf, who had been staring out of the back windows, turned his head expectantly towards his crewmate. "Pies?" he asked hopefully, shaking his head as Whipstaff pointed out of the window.

As if sensing his oversized comrade's disappointment, he reached over and opened the nearest compartment. "Don't worry though, big fella, there's plenty of ice cream in here." Immediately, a contented smile returned to Oaf's face, as he clapped his hands in approval and trotted over to the treasure chest of frozen treats.

Returning his attention back to the cabin, Marty tried to get a view of the rapidly approaching intersection. "Do we know where we're going? I mean, can we get out of town?"

"But of course," the Locust replied without hesitation. "In order to facilitate the fastest exit to the edge of town, we simply take a right here, then continue on for precisely one point four miles before taking a left, followed by another left, and then—"

Marty raised his hands in an attempt to stem the verbal torrent that he had called forth. "Okay, excellent. Let's step on it, then."

Timbers, who had his head out of the passenger side window, returned to his seat, patting Marty's arm urgently. "Never mind stepping on it, we may need to jump up and down on it. We've got company. Look." He pointed at the passenger side wing mirror, from which Marty could see two dark, bounding shapes gaining on them.

Three pogo stick mounted sedans, identical to the one that had literally crashed their party at Stellar Island, jolted and bounced up the road behind them. His mind already whirling, Marty turned sharply to the Locust who seemed oblivious to the pursuit and might just as well have been on a Sunday afternoon boat ride, sitting at the wheel with a jovial grin on his face.

"Excuse me, Mr. Locust. Can we go any faster? They're right behind us."

The wizened old crime fighter gazed up at Marty over his spectacles. "I'm afraid not, young man, taking into consideration the various turns and deviations we will be making, this is the vehicle's maximum safe velocity."

Shaking his head, while at least particularly relieved at getting the short answer for once, Marty met Timbers' stare and took a deep, defiant breath.

"Looks like we're going to have to repel boarders." The little pirate growled, clearly wishing he still had his cutlass.

Marty nodded, moving into the back of the van as he did so. "It looks that way. All hands to battle stations?"

Timbers chuckled into his hand. "I can't believe you just said that. Talk about cheesy."

Marty flushed slightly. "Really? It seemed like a piratey thing to say."

"It'll do just fine," agreed the little pirate, still smirking, but adding an encouraging thumbs up. "Lads! Oh, and… erm…girly," he hollered into the back of the van, tipping his hat as he mentioned Kate. "We've got incoming. What have we got by way of artillery?"

Almost in answer to the question, Oaf turned from the ice cream cabinet, his arms laden with iced lollies, choc ices, and snow cones. Timbers turned back to Marty, meeting his broad grin with an even wider, more mischievous one of his own as the same thought crystalized in both their minds.

"Open the back doors."

The street was still oppressively gloomy and filled with tattered transients as the ice cream van of escapees roared around the corner, blasting a combination of screeching tires and "Greensleeves" in a tumultuous symphony of noise and velocity. Catching a pile of boxes and sending them toppling like garbage filled dominoes, it carried the wave of carnage with it up the street. All too close behind them, their bounding pursuers lurched through the scattered debris and between cowering vagrants, sending a group of wooden cages shattering to the floor in their wake. Freed from their cells, the canaries swooped upwards into the bruised evening sky amid squawking cries for worms and a single tweeting plea for cheese.

Back at street level, the bouncing sedans were gaining on their prey. Through the rear windows of the van, Marty could see the occupants of the chasing vehicles, gibbering and grinning as they closed.

Turning towards his companions, he placed a hand on the door. "Is everybody ready?"

Kate, Whipstaff and Oaf stood in a line, clutching various frozen confectionary and nodding an affirmative.

Beside them, Timbers stood shoulders deep in the freezer cabinet. He tossed out a choc ice to Marty, signaling that he, too, was ready. Marty caught it in one hand and turned the handle with the other, pushing the doors open and bracing himself against the frame as the van drifted erratically around another corner.

Even as they straightened into the next street, the cars behind were upon them, and Marty instinctively ducked, bellowing back into the van as he did so. "Let 'em have it!"

Thirty feet behind them, a freakish clown face poked out of the passenger side window of the lead sedan. Giggling balefully, it glared first at the open doors of the van, then at the figures within the fleeing vehicle, and finally at an arcing, sailing, approaching object. Realizing too late the latter was in fact a Strawberry Screamer, painted face and fruity missile collided with a wet *thud* that sent the demented joker toppling from the car and rolling to a distant, disheveled heap on the roadside.

Kate wound in her pitching arm as the others looked on in awe, before laughter and cheering signified it had indeed been a hell of a shot. The sedans, however, continued to bear down on them, and Marty found a moment to catch Kate's eye, offering his own smiling nod of admiration before turning to open fire. Launching his choc ice at the onrushing freaks, he flinched as a Citrus Monster and a Chocolate Spanker flew past his head, hitting the windscreen of one of the sedans and causing it to swerve and fishtail wildly. Glancing over his shoulder, Marty watched as each of his companions was reloaded by Timbers, who still sat in the freezer to deliver fresh, frozen ammunition as quickly as it was dispatched through the back doors.

"How much more do we have, Timbers?" Marty shouted over the growl of the van's engine.

The little captain glanced down into the freezer in which he sat, rummaging and rustling as he did so. "Plenty. Do you want a Banana Surprise?"

Marty raised an eyebrow, quickly following it up with a cheeky grin. It was a grin that would not have been present that very morning, but one he had quickly learned from Timbers. One that was never out of place no matter the situation. Even in the face of dire peril, there was always time for a sly chuckle at something that sounded a bit naughty.

A heavy crunch just behind him forced the smile from Marty's face. Turning back to the doors, his eyes widened as a clown sedan clattered into the back of the ice cream van a second time, causing it to sway and swerve dangerously. Marty found himself clutching at thin air, but more specifically, the thin air between the back of the ice cream van and the front of the lead sedan. Looping in one fluid movement out of the van, Marty hovered suspended in the air, watching the approaching windscreen and the giggling lunatics behind it. Finally, he came to rest in a sprawling heap on the bonnet of the leaping sedan, grasping for purchase as it lurched skywards once more.

Marty sailed upwards through the air, an unwilling passenger on the vaulting clown car, dimly aware of the hoots and cackles only inches from his face on the other side of the windscreen. As they descended once more, a second demonic sedan drew up alongside, matching both the velocity and trajectory of the lead car.

Marty rose shakily to his feet as a Blueberry Blitz

and a Vanilla Disaster exploded deliciously on the bonnet beside him. The passenger door of the second car opened and a forest of grasping, white gloved hands snaked their way to where Marty stood. With nowhere to run, he glanced back up at the van, spying Timbers as the little pirate leaned out of the side window.

Hefting a large plastic tub, he caught his hat as it threatened to shoot off in the whipping wind. "Typical!" he barked as he dumped the contents of the tub over the side of the van. "All set up for an awesome pun, and I've got nothing."

Neapolitan ice cream cascaded from the side window of the van and flew in huge, lumpy torrents underneath the second sedan. As it dropped into the creamy goop that coated the road, it skewed wildly sideways, the probing hands falling away from where Marty stood exposed. The car spun and skittered across the road, toppling end over end until it was just a smoldering array of twisted metal in the retreating distance of the now triumphant and cheering Timbers.

The Locust shifted gears sharply, and the van dove into a side street, causing the car on which Marty was balanced to pitch in midair and bounce alongside.

Spying his chance, Marty dropped to his haunches. In no conceivable reality did he ever imagine he would be riding a pogo stick propelled gangster wagon full of psychotic clowns, anticipating a possible death defying leap into an ice cream van piloted by a geriatric and a bunch of pirates. And yet here he was, attempting that very feat. Drawing level with the van, his heart leapt as a hand reached out from the side window. It was Kate's, and even before he knew what was happening, Marty was holding out his own hand, reaching to grasp hers. He let himself believe adrenaline had caused his heart to skip a beat, but in truth, it was her hand that he had hoped for, and her hand he now reached for.

Swinging past at a speed that would have made a certain red caped superhero pull on the parking brake, their hands connected, and Kate hauled Marty back into the van. Sprawling inwards to safety, Marty's mind spun through several thousand words to convey his thanks, his smile ultimately giving voice to those words. Kate's eyes managed a bashful 'You're welcome' as a barrage of Cherry Tsunamis blazed past them and peppered the chasing car. It snaked wildly, blinded by the mass of pink mulch, which a pair of ineffective wipers spread thickly across the windscreen.

In the front of the van, the Locust again wrenched the wheel to the left as another intersection split the road ahead. Marty shielded Kate as a box of cones dropped from a shelf above them, breaking open and sending its contents skittering out and into the street behind them. Flying blind in their cherry-coated sedan, the clowns in the lead car sped on. Oblivious to the fact the van they were pursuing had made a sharp left turn, they launched at full speed through the boarded windows of what used to be a large department store.

Peering out of the side window, Timbers let out another whooping cheer as the car disappeared into the building. "That's two down." He declared excitedly. "Where did the other one go?"

Almost in reply to the question, the third sedan appeared menacingly behind him, springing from a side street and screeching up alongside them. It slammed into the side of the van, sending Timbers pitching out of the freezer cabinet and the others staggering to regain their balance. From where he had landed, Timbers peered up at the side window just as a brightly bewigged head poked through, leering crazily in at them. Its horrifically crooked teeth chattered as it cackled. White gloved hands with black, pointed fingernails poking from their ends gripped the sides of the window as the deathly harlequin attempted to slither into the van. Again, time seemed to slow, as it maddeningly tends to when something needs to be done quickly and decisively.

Marty glanced at his companions. Kate seemed rooted to the spot, a look of surprise and terror across her face. Whipstaff was holding up his hands, shaking his head and backing away, and in the cabin, the Locust nodded his head absently, whistling something jolly and carefree. Marty turned to Oaf just as the pint sized giant drifted past him. Gliding through the air with all the grace and poise of a beach ball in a tumble dryer, Oaf had taken the large wooden mallet off his back and angled towards the freak in the window in slow motion. With time to assess his actions, Oaf's expression turned from intrepid determination to dawning panic as he floated closer to his horrifying target. Clearly he had not thought this far ahead, and the slowing of time had given him the opportunity to take stock of what a reckless and foolhardy idea this had been.

Oaf closed his eyes as he reached the window, the claws now reaching out for him, the grin parting to reveal even more jagged teeth. With eyes still closed, he swung his hands up in a wide arc, dragging the mallet up in a sweeping motion that carried it into the face of the despicable jester. With more of a honk than a thud, a red nose looped up and over Oaf's shoulder, landing in Timbers' lap, the diminutive captain having spent the entire chaotic event sitting on the floor at the foot of the freezer. Time seemed to slip back into its usual pace, sending the nose's owner cartwheeling out the window and sprawling across the bonnet of the sedan. Oaf had continued his heroic, if ill-conceived flight, but stopped short of the window, landing instead in the freezer, and sending plumes of icy shards into the air.

Timbers jumped to his feet, still holding his nasal trophy and chuckling to himself. "Thar she nose. Eh? Eh?" The lack of acknowledgement seemed to sully his mood, and he tossed the crimson hooter out to join its owner. "Yeah, all right." He growled. "They can't all be zingers."

Poking his head out of the freezer, Oaf shook the

frost from his hair and blinked. A brief, dazed expression fell away to be replaced by a broad grin. Reaching up from the cabinet in which he sat, he held a choc ice aloft, celebrating his discovery while simultaneously being not entirely sure how he had got there.

With no time for delicious frozen confectionery, Marty was at the window scanning for signs of their single remaining pursuer.

Behind them, several outlandishly pantalooned figures were leaping from the chasing sedan onto the side of the van. From inside the car, through the now shattered windscreen, a pair of huge, unwavering eyes stared back at him. Even though he could see nothing else, Marty knew those eyes belonged to Mr. Peepers. Before the clunking on the roof drew his attention he thought he heard his name whispered, which was of course impossible over the bellowing engines. Nonetheless, he had heard it, and Peepers had said it. The icicle where his spine used to be confirmed that.

Mr. Peepers' smile now appeared, widening so impossibly that Marty half expected the top of his head to fall off. It may well have done so as Marty lost sight of him behind the plastic sliding window that Timbers slammed shut, and brought him back to the closest thing to reality on offer.

The scuffing, scrambling sounds were on all sides of the van, as well as the roof, and it was impossible to say how many giggling interlopers were now on board. Marty took that as a sign that there was 'too many' and raced into the cabin.

The Locust turned as he entered, seemingly still unaware of the peril that literally surrounded them. He rolled his eyes jovially. "They do seem rather persistent, these fellows, don't they?"

Marty shared an incredulous look with Timbers as the little captain appeared at his side. "Yes, they do, rather. Who would have thought that demented, unstoppable, demonic killer clowns would be so demented and unstoppable?"

The Locust shrugged, either in answer to Marty's question or simple indifference to his rant, which continued unabated regardless.

"I mean, everything here is a construct of my own dreamscape. You would think that somewhere in this van there would be some kind of anti-clown gizmo if it's all come from inside my head."

Timbers tugged at Marty's sleeve, pointing over at the dashboard where a large red button sat prominently next to the radio. "Well, there is," he explained calmly. "I've been pushing that thing for the past few minutes, though I think it's broken."

In the back of the van, white gloved hands reached in through the side hatch, and leering faces peered in through the rear windows. Marty threw panicked glances back and forth, looking for a way out. In a speeding van covered with homicidal clowns, the ideas weren't readily forthcoming. He returned his attention to the Locust, who still focused intently on the road ahead.

From the passenger seat, Timbers interjected once more. "We're nearly at the edge of town. If we can get out into the open, perhaps we could signal for the Fathom?"

"It wouldn't get here in time." replied Marty, shaking his head. "Locust, do you have any suggestions?"

The jumpsuited geriatric seemed to momentarily emerge from his inner little world, raising an eyebrow as though calculating something. Almost immediately, a wry smile hinted across his lips and he nodded. "Given our current predicament and current rate of velocity, I believe that our only remaining logical course of action would be to crash."

Even before Marty and Timbers could reply in tandem, a chorus of disbelief that would outline their extreme disagreement of this hypothesis, the Locust spun the wheel sharply. Teetering onto two wheels briefly, the ice cream van righted and gunned at speed towards a rather solid looking brick wall.

Marty had scarcely enough time to yell, "Hold on to something," before the front windscreen filled with the image of the approaching wall, and then exploded.

Having had some brief forewarning of the imminent collision, Marty stopped short of exiting the vehicle via the front window as it blasted spectacularly through the brick wall. He flapped and swung from the doorway to the rear of the van, but mercifully remained in a position of relative safety. Relative that was to the half dozen clownish shapes that pitched into view ahead of them as they were flung from their perch atop the crashing vehicle. Clearly, they had not seen the oncoming obstruction and were now sailing through the air like grinning rag dolls as first debris, and then the parts of van, followed them through the gaping hole that had been masonry moments earlier.

Behind him, Marty was dimly aware of the chaos of flailing limbs and cries of panic of his companions. While Kate struggled to stay upright, Whipstaff and Oaf cartwheeled crazily about the toppling van. In the cabin, Timbers had dived into the foot well and was rattling around like a pea in a whistle as they tilted and began to roll sideways. In the driver's seat, the Locust was securely belted in place and seemed oblivious to the carnage as the van spun onto its roof, then back onto its wheels. It continued in a crunching, bone-jarring pirouette as the verge beyond the wall gave way to a steep slope.

As the world whirled past in a gut wrenching kaleidoscope outside the window, Marty closed his eyes and counted to ten, hoping by that time they would either be dead or at the bottom of the slope, preferably the latter. He had only reached eight, however, when the van lurched to a wounded rest on its side. As the contents of the van, some of them struggling to keep their lunches down, came to a stop, Marty scanned the interior, taking a mental attendance as he did so. Despite Oaf being lodged head first in a cardboard box, and Kate fishing chocolate sprinkles out of her hair, everyone seemed to be present and in one piece. It was then that Marty realized, although they had come to rest at the bottom of the slope, they were still in fact moving.

Staggering into the back of the van, Marty hoisted himself up to the side hatch, now operating as more of a sun roof, and peered outside.

The gloom and oppression of the city had vanished. Marty squinted at the bright sunlight that filled the sky, and tried to focus. In the receding distance, he could see the breached wall, which surrounded the city, still enveloped in its dark shroud. Wide sweeping furrows were cut into the bank that led from the wall, no doubt caused by their haphazard descent. At the foot of the slope, water lapped against a shoreline, and Marty suddenly realized why they were still moving. Stretching back past the hole in the wall that they made ran a lazily flowing river which carried the van in its current. There was no sign of anything clown related except for a single curly red wig floating alongside them.

Marty ducked his head back inside the hatch. "Hey, there's a river out here. We landed in a river."

"Ahh, that'll be what all this water coming through the windscreen is from then." Timbers' voice replied from the cabin.

His supposition appeared to be accurate, and water gushed across the floor of the van, filling it with alarming rapidly. Wading out from the cabin, Timbers was closely followed by the Locust, who lifted up the tiny captain to keep him from disappearing beneath the rising waters. Kate, Oaf, and Whipstaff clambered into the freezer cabinet, which was now bobbing towards the hatch from where Marty watched.

"We can't stay in here, this van will be underwater any minute," he called down to his paddling comrades.

"Indeed not," the Locust responded, pitching Timbers up at the hole in the roof. "Here, catch this pirate."

Marty obliged, and Timbers sat down next to him, feet dangling over the edge of the hatch as the water slowly rose to meet them. Suddenly struck with an idea, and realizing they would need more than a freezer to float away from this car wreck, Marty leaned over the side of the van, clutching and pulling at something. The something wrenched free, and Marty reappeared, dragging the large plastic cone, which had adorned the roof of the vehicle, behind him.

Timbers snapped his fingers in approval. "I like it. It's not what you'd call traditionally seaworthy, but I like it."

Kate's head rose from the hatch between them, as the water pushed the cabinet out of the sinking van. A pair of green gloved hands followed it, gripping the side of the hatch and hauling the wiry form of the Locust out to join them. Nimbly, the aged crime fighter hopped onto the floating cone that was now being piloted by Marty and Timbers. The top of the van drifted beneath the water as the cabinet popped up alongside them. Marty made a grab for it, relieved to see that it still contained two pirates. He was even more relieved Kate was still sitting with them. Blowing hair out of his eyes, Marty shot her a smile borne partly from the exhilaration of both survival and escape, but mainly from the fact that she was smiling just as broadly.

"Well, it's not exactly a romantic boat ride." He shrugged, still beaming.

She hardly skipped a beat before replying. "It certainly beats being chased by clowns, but if this was a date, you'd be in trouble."

Timbers chuckled, jabbing Marty with a clothy finger. "Look, if you're going to just sit here and flirt, you can get off my ship."

"This isn't a ship." Marty pointed out. "It's a giant ice cream cone."

"Yes, yes it is." Timbers straightened his coat and placed his hands on his hips. "And it's mine. I'll have no talk of mutiny on my cone."

Marty's grin remained, and he turned to Timbers, casually knocking the tiny captain's hat off and delivering a mock salute. Timbers caught the hat before it hit the water and shot Marty a look. It was an expression tempered with amusement and mirth, which was quickly put to one side as he turned to address the Locust.

"So, we made it out, and we find ourselves, albeit a little damp, in a fortuitous position." He glanced back at Marty, pointing as he did so at the green suited pensioner beside them. "The Locust here is quite the bookworm, shall we say. Shall we also say that he knows a thing or two about a thing or two. I'll bet you doubloons to doughnuts that he knows how you can get home."

Marty blinked, taking in that last statement and regarding the amiable old fellow who sat beside him, peering out happily from behind his spectacles. Finally he arranged his thoughts in the correct order and gave voice to them. "Do you? Do you know how I can get out of here and back to where I belong?"

The Locust raised his eyebrows, leaning closer to Marty and patting him on the shoulder. "My dear fellow, I haven't got a clue."

A moment of silence passed between them as the response that everyone had expected failed to materialize, replaced instead by a rather awkward shrug of the shoulders.

Timbers broke the silence with the sort of overblown gusto that one would expect from a pirate. "What? You're supposed to be this big know it all, and the one question we ask you, that we actually need an answer to, you've got nothing." He reached for his cutlass before remembering it wasn't there, settling instead for an industrial strength scowl.

The Locust raised his hands in a calming notion. "My friend, you don't understand. My knowledge stretches the length and breadth of this land. I can tell you how long it would take to get from one end to the other on a pogo stick. I can tell you how often the cheeseburger trees need watering. I can even tell you how to hotwire one of the mechanical pandas. This, however, all takes place within the confines of your dream. If you want to know how to get out, you will need to speak to the Book Keeper."

Pausing, as if to add weight and dramatic effect to his speech, the Locust spotted the blank expressions staring back at him, and continued. "The Book Keeper is in charge of the comings and goings. He will, undoubtedly, have the answers you require. And as luck would have it, we are pointed in the right direction already. If you follow this river to its source, you will find him." Rising to his feet, he put his hands together and bowed slightly. "I wish you the best of luck and farewell."

Marty frowned, glancing at Timbers as the pint sized buccaneer leapt to his feet. "Wait, you're leaving? You've come this far with us. You can't leave now." he beseeched.

The Locust turned to face Timbers, kneeling to eye level. "I'm afraid it's one rescue per customer, so you're already one over quota. And besides, as his name suggests, the Book Keeper…well, he keeps books. That's off limits for me. He doesn't like me nibbling on his collection, you see." The old man's face softened as he gestured towards Marty and the others in the freezer cabinet. "You'll be fine. You're back with your friends and heading in the right direction. My work here is done."

Timbers nodded forlornly, shaking the green gloved hand extended towards him. Without speaking another word, the Locust launched himself high into the air, turning an impressive somersault as he dropped salmon-like into the water, vanishing without a trace.

Marty placed a hand on Timbers' shoulder. "Come on. This cone needs its captain."

Timbers giggled. "That doesn't make any sense," he replied, before trotting over to the front of the makeshift ship.

Marty rolled his eyes. "Everything that's happened today and *that* doesn't make sense?" He managed a half-suppressed chuckle.

Nodding, Timbers turned and barked out orders to his crew in the cabinet alongside. "Right, men, get these two craft secured together. It seems we're off to the library."

All things considered, and after everything that had happened that day, the boat ride seemed almost serene. Certainly a pleasant distraction and, at the very least, a welcome breather. Marty sat at the head of the giant cone, keeping a firm hold on the freezer cabinet that floated lazily alongside. Squinting as the sun threw shards of brilliant light back up from the sparkling water, he smiled nervously at Kate who sat beside him. Since most of the day had been spent rushing from or to somewhere, there had scarcely been time to think, let alone engage in small talk. Now, with the complete absence of peril bearing down upon them, Marty found himself struggling for something to say.

Back on the lifeboat, he had been full of courageous intent, riding in the wake of the plan he had concocted so the verbal jousting that had occurred had been almost automatic, the very definition of 'winging it.' Here, there was no plan, no real urgency. They were literally meandering towards their destination with no conceivable threat in the vicinity. Of course, this was usually the juncture at which a threat leapt out from nowhere and bit your legs off, but if one spent all of one's time worrying about such things, one wouldn't get very far, Marty reasoned.

Sparing him any further deliberation, uncertainty and philosophical claptrap, Kate broke the silence between them. "So, this isn't too bad, considering, is it?"

Marty smiled, nodding in agreement. "There are certainly worse ways to make a getaway."

She returned her gaze to the water, glancing back at Marty out of the corner of her eye. "Like I said, if this was a date, you'd be in trouble right about now. Crashed ice cream vans don't exactly create a good first impression."

Marty's eyes widened, and he turned to face Kate. She was still studying the water but had allowed a wry smile to play across her face. Searching for a comeback to this unexpected comment, a stifled, nervous laugh was all that was forthcoming.

Realizing she, too, had giggled bashfully at the implication, Kate changed the subject. "So, when you get back, what do you think you'll do?"

Marty paused for a moment before shaking his head slightly. "I don't know. I mean, I can't really tell anyone about this. They'll stick me in a padded cell. I suppose I could write it all down, but I never really was that good with words." He sighed.

Kate leaned towards him, grabbing his hand and giving it a reassuring squeeze. "I think you do better than you think."

Popping up behind Marty, Timbers completely ruined the moment. "I hope I'm not ruining some kind of moment here. It's just that you might want to take a look at this."

As Marty turned to face him, the tiny captain gestured over the side of the cone. "It's the water. It's gone a bit…papery."

Looking down over the side of the cone, a sheet of paper whipped upwards out of nowhere, clinging to Marty's face before the breeze took it skyward. Down where the water used to be, and indeed should still have been, a lapping, swaying torrent of pages swept past. Marty blinked as his mind struggled to process what he was seeing. It was paper, but it was behaving like water, flowing past them and swelling against the sides of their makeshift crafts.

"Will you look at that," Timbers tutted, shaking his head. "A man overboard who drops into that is going to be in paper cut Hell."

More pages fluttered past and dropped into the writhing throng. In fact, more paper seemed to be sweeping into the air as the *water* current became more urgent, carrying the cone and cabinet vessel along faster than ever.

Spying a cluster of rocks and foliage which had spilled out into this literary stream, Timbers decided it was time to disembark. "It's getting a little choppy out here, and I am really not comfortable with sailing on paper anyway. I think we should get back on dry land."

Marty decided to forego the obvious 'land lubber' quip, since he wasn't entirely sure what they were all currently lubbing at the moment, anyway.

Timbers peered over the side again and studied the current as it swirled and ebbed alongside. It looked like water, it sounded like water, and it acted like water. And yet fluttering pages drifted out of the torrent, tossing and rejoining the rest in a singular fluid motion like no waves he had ever seen before. Suitably confused, Marty nodded in agreement to the suggestion, trotting to the front of the cone to make a grab at the passing fauna.

The current grew stronger, and before long they had arrived at the rocks. Marty grabbed the branch of an overhanging tree, bringing the floating convoy to a lurching halt. The cabinet passengers needed no prompting, as first Kate, and then Whipstaff hopped across onto the rocks. Oaf lumbered after them, still holding a choc ice, which he had salvaged from the abandoned freezer. Timbers sprang to his feet, took a run up across the cone and landed deftly next to his companions. Bringing up the rear, Marty hoisted himself up, using the branch for balance, and swung the short distance across to safety. He landed in a scrambling heap, caught by Kate before he slipped back into the papery flume.

He regained his balance, meeting her gaze and smiling appreciatively. "You're making a habit of catching me aren't you?"

Kate smiled cheekily. "You should stop falling for me, then," she replied, winking.

Marty dearly wished he had something witty to reply with and was, for once relieved, when Timbers once again interrupted.

The little captain stood on the tallest rock, which jutted out over the river. "Erm, I think getting off the river here was a good call," he muttered, gazing out to a point obscured by the surrounding rocks. Marty scrambled up to join his miniature companion, standing beside him with his mouth agape at the sight beyond.

The river flowed a further forty or fifty feet, becoming faster and more violent before reaching a crescendo atop an enormous waterfall. Countless pages spilled out over the edge of what would more accurately be called a paper fall, crashing and tumbling into the unseen depths below.

Timbers sighed and turned towards Marty. "Well, what now? The Locust said to go this way, but I left my hang glider and suicidal tendencies at home."

Marty scratched his head, gazing at the turbulent paper maelstrom. "Maybe we can take a less plummetty route," he pondered out loud, pointing to the river bank to the right of the cascade.

Almost completely obscured behind a cluster of bushes, lay a roughhewn dirt track, which wound towards the edge of the paper fall and disappeared from view beside it. It was almost indistinguishable but clearly led somewhere, and since Marty had also left his hang glider at home, it seemed to be the only way forward.

Hopping off the outcrop, Marty motioned for his companions to follow and headed for the path. With Timbers close behind, and Kate already catching up to them both, Whipstaff turned to Oaf, who was wringing his hands worriedly.

"What's the matter, big lad?" the first mate enquired.

"I haven't brought a hang glider either," Oaf whimpered, pulling a small white handkerchief from his pocket. "I suppose I could use this as a parachute."

Whipstaff chuckled and patted his bumbling shipmate on the shoulder. "Don't fret, lad, I think we're taking the scenic route." He pointed to the dirt track Marty had nearly reached.

Oaf brightened, returning the handkerchief to his pocket. "Oh, that's much better," he boomed, relief ringing loudly in his voice. "I can eat my choc ice on the way down." Happily, he unwrapped his frozen treasure as the pair trotted over to the dirt track to join their friends.

Soon, the group was all present and accounted for, peering into what appeared to be a deep and lush fissure. Cascading into it, the paper fall plunged into unseen depths below, crashing against dense and vibrant foliage. The pathway on which they stood took a more leisurely descending route, wending its way in a twisting spiral around the plummeting paper to a point where it was almost undetectable in the distance.

Timbers hitched up his belt and turned to his

companions. "Well, looks like we've got some walking to do. If anybody is interested, I will be doing requests." With that, he dove into a jolly sounding sea shanty that seemed to involve a lusty serving wench and a bucket of custard.

Marty turned to Kate and shrugged, before holding his hand out in a gentlemanly 'ladies first' gesture. Smiling, she fell in behind the inappropriately warbling captain, with Marty close behind on the narrow track. Whipstaff and Oaf brought up the rear, the former joining in the chorus with vigor while the latter merely giggled at the subject matter of the song.

So narrow was the path, in fact, single file was the only option as they made their descent, sheer cliff face on one side, sheer drop and the roaring paper fall on the other. Peering over the side nervously, Marty could see little past the dropping reams of paper and overgrown vegetation, but continued to keep pace with the bawdy tune that was bellowed from the front of the line. It had changed and seemed to mainly pertain to an unfortunate mariner who had lost his way in a multi-story car park. The tone was still energetic, however, and so the pace remained brisk.

Still marching in time with the ditty, Kate shot a glance over her shoulder. "So, what do you think we'll find at the bottom?" she asked over what appeared to be a new song about a drunken bar fight between a fisherman and an enraged dolphin.

Marty hadn't thought that far ahead, having already spent most of the day riding the crest of half-baked plans and hastily conceived ideas. "I'm not sure," he began, biting his thumbnail thoughtfully. "A lot of paper, that's for sure."

A flurry of pages swept by them as they passed closer to the edge to avoid a particularly uneven patch of thicket obscuring the path. Marty flung his hand out instinctively and caught a sheet as it fluttered past, plucking it from the air to give closer inspection. There was writing on it, and Marty stopped to bring the sheet close enough to read it.

At the front, Timbers simultaneously came to a halt as he sensed the pause in their progress. "Why have we stopped?" He trotted back to where Marty and Kate stood. "Does someone need to use the toilet?"

Marty was studying the paper in his hand, his brow furrowed as he struggled to comprehend what he was looking at. There was writing on the page. Writing that seemed to form a list.

—The names of the two stone lions in front of the New York Public Library are Patience and Fortitude. They were named by then-mayor Fiorello LaGuardia.

—The king of hearts is the only king in the deck without a moustache.

—The plastic things on the end of shoelaces are called aglets.

—Ancient Greeks believed that ginger haired people would turn into vampires after their deaths.

The list continued to the bottom of the page, and looking back at the cascading deluge of pages, Marty could see that they were all similarly scribed. "It doesn't make sense. What is all this?" he murmured absently, almost to himself.

Timbers snatched the paper from his hands and scanned it. "Ha ha! Gingers," he chuckled upon reaching the bottom of the page. "You're right, it doesn't make much sense, but they're all heading one way." The little pirate pointed down into the depths of the fissure. "It's a safe bet that we'll find some answers down there." Timbers spun on his heels and swung a beckoning hand out behind him. "Come on. Last one to the bottom has to do Oaf's laundry." With that, he returned to singing and marching, striking up a rather heartfelt ditty about a mermaid who dreams of being a real girl and ends up in a can of tuna.

Thanks largely to Timbers' impressive repertoire, the single file line made significant progress into the belly of the fissure. The chamber seemed to open out and provide the group with a little more room as they hiked ever downwards. The paper fall, which fell incessantly beside them, seemed to expand and increase in ferocity as they descended, taking up more and more room as the gap around it widened. Conversely, the dense undergrowth, which had formed a carpet on the pathway, had subsided somewhat. Where it had earlier hampered the group's journey along the track, it now hung in intricate patterns and seemed to yield to them as they made their way down.

Passing a sinewy vine branch, Kate paused to push it out of the way. As she did so, a more regimented, almost manmade array of vines were revealed beneath. Furthermore, in amongst them hung what appeared to be a long row of books. Marty arrived at her side as she hauled the covering vines to one side to reveal a natural shelf, filled from one side to the other with books of various sizes and thicknesses. She raised an incredulous eyebrow and a disbelieving glance towards Marty, who returned fire with a confused expression of his own. With curiosity now pushing them onward, they quickened their pace, catching up with Timbers, who was now warbling about a mutiny that had broken out amongst a crew who had run out of sea shanties to sing.

Casting suspicious glances at the leafy walls as they descended, Marty and Kate spied more books housed within the shelf like fronds of the surrounding vegetation, which seemed to resemble mighty sweeping bookcases with every step they continued to take.

The sound sprang up from beneath them before they even saw the bottom of the fissure. Rather than the crashing roar of rushing water, the paper arrived at its terminus with a whooshing flurry that sounded more like a newspaper stand caught in a twister. The noise swelled to a crescendo as the pathway finally opened into a clearing, and what was presumably the bottom of the fissure.

The pathway snaked to a gradual stop at a stretch of lush but overgrown grassland. It spread out in a wide circle, itself encompassing a large pool into which the torrential paper fall flowed. Although they must have been a few hundred meters down, sunlight flooded the chamber, weaving in amongst the descending paper and casting dancing beams of light onto the ground like reflections from an enormous glitter ball.

Marty stepped into the clearing, taking in the ambience and tranquillity of his undeniably idyllic surroundings. It had all the hallmarks of a paper enthusiast's happy place but was clearly impressing the members of the group who thought paper was *only* okay.

The pirates trotted into the center of the field, chuckling and chasing each other in the flickering sunlight, while Marty looked on, happy, for once, shenanigans were taking precedence over immediate horrific peril. He sat down in the cool, dense grass and squinted into the breach from which they had just arrived. It looked a lot bigger from the bottom and an awful lot higher. It was easy to see how this place could be so untouched, and so unnoticed, by the world above. As he sat immersed in his daydreams, a hand dropped onto Marty's shoulder. Kate stood at his side and was now pulling at his arm, urging him to his feet.

Rising, Marty's brow creased as he noticed the expression on her face as she stared intently at a point somewhere behind him. "Kate, what is it?" He turned to see what had caught her attention.

Bordering the field, and stretching upwards on all sides, vines intertwined and contorted to form roughhewn walls. More vines and branches grew across these walls to form impossibly straight and structured shelves, upon which countless leather bound books sat in swirling rows that ran the full circle of the clearing. Soaring up until they merged with the natural growth from above, this resplendent library reached skywards towards the sunlight and housed more dusty volumes than it would be possible to count.

"Wow, look at that." Timbers gazed up at the perpetually ascending tomes. "There must be a thousand books up there. Ten thousand."

Oaf loped over to the nearest shelf and held out a finger. "One, two, three, four, five…" he began before Whipstaff appeared at his side, grabbing the scanning digit and shaking his head at the tiny giant. "Shhhh, Oaf. There's lots, so let's just leave it at that."

"Lots is an understatement," a voice interrupted. It seemed to come from everywhere at once, echoing off the walls, and stopping everyone in their tracks. "In fact, you might say that there are more books here that you could possibly read in a lifetime."

The ground appeared to shake as this new voice cannoned forth from nowhere, even though it was even, mellow, and soothing. Marty scanned the field for signs of another presence before the voice spoke again, this time seemingly from within the walls. "You're here to find a way out aren't you? The Locust sent you."

Timbers joined Marty, scanning the scene for signs of the mysterious new presence. "It's a ghost. Look, I'm no coward, but I think we should definitely run away screaming," he whispered, edging back towards the path.

Ignoring his pint-sized comrade, Marty stepped forward, addressing the ether in front of him. "Erm, yes.

The Locust sent us here to find a way for me to get home." His voice carried a determined tone he was starting to like.

Something shifted in the corner of his eye, and Marty turned to scrutinize the flanking wall of books. Although nothing seemed to immediately present itself, the shelves appeared to ripple as the voice spoke again. "Interesting. Not that interesting, though." The disembodied voice emitted a long, drawn out yawn that sent a few books toppling from their lofty perches. "I tell you what," the voice continued. "Why don't we play a little game? If you win, I'll tell you what you want to know."

Marty threw up his hands in frustration. "Of course! Nothing as simple as a signpost with 'Way Out' written on it, now we have to play twenty questions!" Stopping mid-rant, he sighed, composing himself as Timbers appeared at his side.

"Pardon me. What if we lose?" the little captain asked.

The voice tutted. "If you lose, you get to go away, leave me in peace and find your own way home."

Turning to Kate and shrugging, Marty addressed the bookshelves once more. "All right then, I suppose we have no choice."

More books tumbled from their lofty housings as laughter whooshed down through the fissure like some kind of amused wind. "Excellent!" the voice exclaimed as the laughing subsided. "All you have to do is answer a simple question, and I'll tell you anything you want to know."

Timbers turned back towards Marty, a familiar grin

had returned to his face. "We've got this." he winked. "One question? This'll be a walk on the plank."

Cutting the miniature swashbuckler off, the voice spoke again, sending soaring, swooping words rushing through the ether. Vines and trees rustled and bent as they blasted imposingly around the clearing. The question was short, direct, and contained only three words.

"Who. Am. I?"

As Marty exchanged glances with his comrades, he became aware that a good few moments had passed since the question had been delivered. These moments had been filled with an awkward and vacuous silence, which seemed to suck in the surrounding ambient noises and muffle them. Searching for something to say to allay this sound vortex, Marty managed only a vague and stalling, "Pardon?"

"Who am I?" The voice asked again. "It's a simple question, and in time honored tradition, I will give you three guesses. Unlike the great Sphinx however, if you get it wrong, I will not devour you. Probably." Again, whirling laughter spun stray pages in aerial pirouettes and rattled books on their shelves.

Marty turned to his companions, a smile spreading across his face. *Surely it couldn't be this easy?* he thought. "The Locust already told us, you're the Book Keeper."

An irritated *tch!* echoed around the clearing, as the voice retorted. "No, no, no. That is the name I have been given. One is not defined by how he is viewed by others. A name is just a name." The philosophical monologue relented slightly, "I'm sorry, maybe I should have been more specific. I want you to tell me who I *am*, not what names I am known by. You can have that guess as a practice. A do over."

Although imposing, the tone seemed jovial and benevolent, and Marty decided it was most likely telling the truth; at least about not devouring them. The worrying part, however, was the actual logic, perception, deduction, or in this case, blind guesswork that would now have to be undertaken. He turned towards Kate, who was eyeing the bookcases quizzically. Next to her, Timbers was stroking his whiskery chin thoughtfully, while further past them, in the field, Whipstaff and Oaf bounced past, midway through an impromptu game of leapfrog.

Turning back towards the center of the clearing, and taking a few steps towards the fluttering paper fall, Marty searched deep within himself for something that resembled a decent answer. It was clear the denizen of the bookcases was unlike anything he had ever encountered before, but given how his day had panned out, that counted for very little. Taking the day's exploits into consideration, they might just as well be addressing a giant inflatable beaver who was also the chairman of the National Pro Celebrity Tiddlywinks Championship. Good sense fought back the urge to use that as his first proper guess, presenting him with a far less insane option.

Before he could give voice to it however, a smaller one spoke up from behind him. "It's clearly a public address system for some sort of massive jungle library tour, right?" Timbers chipped in confidently.

Before Marty could turn to face his tiny compadre, their unseen host bellowed out a gusty reply. "I'm sorry, but that is not correct." It sounded almost apologetic. Marty peered over his shoulder to where Timbers stood next to Kate. The little captain's eye had widened and both cloth hands were up to his mouth as he hopped from one foot to the next.

He whispered a sheepish, "Sorry," through his cupped hands as Marty nodded and held up a hand. With the other, he pressed a finger to his lips in an 'It's ok, but shhh!' gesture.

Trying to calm himself, and focus his thoughts, Marty returned his attention to the cascading paper fall, the swelling pool below it, and the towering bookshelves above. How could he possibly make sense of this? None of these things belonged together, and it made his head hurt just to think about it.

Arriving at his side, Kate placed a hand on his shoulder. "So, what do you think?" she asked, her tone as doubtful as his train of thought.

"I honestly have no idea," he replied shakily, staring at his hands. "I don't even know where to begin."

Kate's tone seemed to brighten, as though she sensed he needed the positivity. "It's a case of deduction. It can't be that hard to figure out, we just have to look at the facts we have."

Marty looked up, pondering this approach. Her logic was sound, and they really didn't have anything else to go on. "All right, so what do we have?" he mused. "This guy's obviously some kind of big deal. He's got a nice place here, away from all the panic and chasing and peril and such. And he's being sent a lot of information via the waterfall thingy." Raising a hand to grab Kate's on his shoulder, he gave it a squeeze and crowed triumphantly. "I think I've got it!"

He took a step closer to the pool, the smile returning to his face. It all made sense, when he looked at things on their own like that. It was so obvious, he almost laughed out loud at not having the foresight to see it sooner. Positioning himself prominently upon a raised knoll, and standing proudly, hands on hips and chest puffed out, Marty shouted his guess with a new found assuredness. "I think that, you sir, are the boss here. You run the show. You're like a director. A conductor. A supervisor. It may come from my head, but it plays out according to your rules."

Taking a step back, Marty squinted upwards into the jaggedly intruding sunlight, smiling contentedly as he awaited the response.

"That's a very well-reasoned and concisely worded answer," the voice rang out encouragingly from above. "It's also completely wrong, but still, very impressive. One guess left."

Sinking to his knees, Marty stared in disbelief out over the papery waters of the pool, and upwards through the swirling sheets into the sparkling sunlight overhead. How could he have been wrong? It seemed to all fit. It seemed a dead certainty. He felt as though all of his deductive reasoning had been ploughed into that answer and he had nothing more to contribute. With one more guess to go, Marty scarcely had the wherewithal to even come up with a random possibility. The giant inflatable beaver was starting to seem like a viable, and indeed, his only other option, which was a shame because he really wasn't convinced that answer was entirely feasible.

Obviously, the paper would be easier to dam, and should the big fella run out of wood, he could always use…paper, but there were also splinters to consider, the natural enemy of the inflatable. No, it just didn't add up, but then again, guess number two had added up perfectly and had been a resounding 'Close, but no cigar.'

As these and a thousand more rabid unfettered thoughts threatened to derail Marty's train of thought, a stray sheet of the paper fall swept downwards, dancing through the air and departing from its rustling brethren. It swooped and twirled, end over end before coming to rest squarely across Marty's face. Reaching up to remove it, he glanced at the writing, which formed yet another list across the page.

—*The Aztecs were the first people to serve chocolate as a drink.*
—*'Almost' is the longest word in the English language with*

all the letters in alphabetical order.

—There is a town in North Carolina called Boogertown.

Marty stared at the paper, his brow furrowed and his eyes fixed on one line. "I've heard this somewhere before." he muttered, almost to himself. "I remember hearing this. I remember laughing about it with everyone in the pub." An eyebrow rose as he got to his feet, pacing closer to the pool as he did so. "It was one of the questions in the pub quiz. It was a question none of us knew the answer to. We laughed about it all night, but I'd completely forgotten about it until now."

Leaning towards the crashing paper fall, he swiped at the flowing pages, snagging another and scanning the list upon it.

—Chewing gum leads to flatulence as you swallow more air as you chew.

"I know this as well!" Marty exclaimed, becoming visibly more excited. "I read this at school and ended up eating ten packs in one go." He glanced over at Kate, flushing slightly. "I wanted to see if I could set a world record."

Returning his attention back to the page, he continued to read. "All this, everything written here, they're all things I've heard or read at some point. It's like a list of my memories."

Marty looked up, meeting Kate's gaze as he did. The same thing that had suddenly dawned on him was clearly etched on her face, and she nodded an excited recognition of the fact as he faced the mighty bookshelves once more.

"Excuse me," he began, almost afraid to start down this road, but at the same time more confident than ever of its destination. "I think I'm ready to give you my final guess."

The voice within the soaring shelves sounded almost as excited as Marty himself felt. Clearly it was as eager to hear this final, make or break answer as Marty was to deliver it. "Oh, yes? Excellent. The best of luck to you," it boomed with an air of almost palpable sincerity.

"Okay, I'm not going to beat about the bush. You clearly have a lot of information coming through here." Marty pointed at the plummeting pages. "And you keep it all stored here, in this outrageously huge library of books."

Whipstaff, who had finished his game of leapfrog with Oaf, leaned in towards Timbers. "I thought he said he wasn't going to beat about the bush? He's going on a bit," the little first mate whispered.

Timbers responded with an abrupt, "Shh!" as Marty continued.

"The fact that all these snippets of information are so random and yet still things that I have heard of points to only one thing." Pausing for dramatic effect, he glanced at his friends, who were clearly not giving points for presentation. Timbers peered at a pocket watch while Oaf delved in his pockets in search of some mystery item. Sensing he was losing the crowd, Marty got to the point.

"You, my friend, are my subconscious."

The silence that descended went on for some moments, as though the owner of the voice was checking a manual or rulebook, and Marty shifted uncertainly where he stood, beginning to feel the second guesses slithering up in his mind. Presently, though, the silence was broken by what sounded like thunder. Several violent thunderclaps shook the sky, and the group shrank down onto their haunches away from the deafening reports. As it continued, however, Marty realized it wasn't thunder they were hearing. It was applause. Mighty applause from the heavens, or more accurately, from the imposing bookshelves, which shook and dropped more of their contents into the field below.

"Very good! You are correct, sir!" The voice enthused happily between amidst the thunderous applause. "As you rightly pointed out, everything you come into contact with, facts, information, songs, quotes—all of it—gets flung down into your subconscious. You remember everything. You just don't remember you remember."

Almost before Marty could exhale the sigh of relief that was clamoring to escape, his friends were upon him. Timbers landed on his back, laughing and crowing as Oaf and Whipstaff joined the celebratory assault. Marty buckled as the pirates landed, falling forward into the grass and allowing the relief to giggle out of him.

Watching from where she stood, Kate smiled broadly, coughing slightly to catch Marty's attention. "So, how did you guess that?"

Marty smiled back at her and sat up, two pirates in a headlock and one on his shoulders. "It was just like you said. I just looked at everything for what it is." He gestured towards the paper fall before them. "All this information comes into my subconscious like a torrent, like a waterfall, and then it all gets stored up there in dusty old bookshelves, out of sight and out of mind."

Kate shook her head, still smiling and added her own, much less earth shaking applause. "I am impressed." She beamed, sharing as much of a moment as one can with someone wrestling tiny pirates.

As the revelry subsided, Marty got to his feet and made his way back over to Kate. "So, now what?" she enquired, gazing back up towards the shelves.

"Yes," Marty echoed, once more addressing the voice from above. "What now?"

"Now?" his subconscious replied softly, clearly pleased that they had passed its test. "Now, you're going to have to catch a train."

"Perhaps I should elaborate," the subconscious added, after enough time and silence had passed to suggest that some elaboration was required. More words spilled forth, rustling the undergrowth and sending a breeze through the clearing. The tone seemed lighter and less imposing now. "You seem to have a handle on how things work here, so what I am about to tell you won't be too hard to understand."

Marty felt a twinge of pride creep up inside him. His own subconscious had given him a compliment, and although this would take some time to get his head around, it was nice to know he appreciated himself.

Unabated, the voice from above continued. "As you are no doubt aware, this place and everything in it is a construct of your own dream space. A very…interesting place I think you'll agree."

"Interesting? Yes, but altogether too clowny for my liking," Marty interjected. "It's not exactly a vacation spot," he added, angling a, "No offense," at Timbers out of the corner of his mouth."

"Hey, it's your mind, matey. I only work here," Timbers retorted, sticking out his tongue and giggling gruffly.

If the voice of Marty's subconscious had a throat, he cleared it now, sending rumblings around the clearing and retrieving the attention of everyone present. "Anyway, it's clear you wish to leave, and there is a way."

Timbers tugged at Marty's leg. "Ooh, there you go. I bet this is where we have to catch a train," he chirped excitedly.

Oaf, who was stood next to Whipstaff behind them, kicked a stone and muttered something about how he got sick on trains.

"If I could just have your attention for one moment," the voice boomed, clearly frustrated by the interruptions. Timbers held up his hands in apology, and Oaf covered his eyes, prompting the subconscious to continue with its explanation.

"As I was saying," it began again after a lengthy sigh. "There is a way for you to leave this place. It lies at the edge of the city. You see, the further you journey from the center of this place, the closer you get to lucidity."

Snapping her fingers, Kate now spoke up. "Ahh! I've heard of this. When you lucid dream, you are aware that you are dreaming. You can shape what you do within the dream, so that makes sense."

"Your friend is correct," the subconscious chipped in, having seemingly given up on challenging the interruptions. "Lucid dreaming is the thinnest point between here and there. Luckily for you, lucid dream space is an actual place here, or to be more precise, a train station."

Attempting to maintain the handle on this that he apparently had, Marty joined in the interruption theme. "Why a train station?"

The subconscious seemed to anticipate Marty's question, which, given their relationship to each other, wasn't overly impressive. "Well, people who lucid dream go wherever they want to in the dream space, and they need a point from which they can journey to whichever place they desire."

Marty raised a finger, clearly in need of further clarification, before remembering the sheer volume of things that had made just as little sense to him today. "So, how do we get there then?" he asked, lowering his now redundant digit.

"Just head north from here," his subconscious answered. "You won't be able to miss Lucidity Junction, mostly because there are trains there."

Marty stepped forward, seeking some sort of

confirmation of what was, it had to be said, something of a cryptic string of instructions. "So let me make sure I have this straight. We need to head to this train station, get on a train, and that'll get me out of here?" Cringing, he glanced back at his comrades. That had sounded almost too ridiculous to be true.

"I know, it sounds almost too ridiculous to be true," his subconscious confirmed. "But as I said, it's the weakest point between where you are and where you want to be. The fact that you want to be there will be enough to see you on your way."

Marty pondered on the idea, trying not to let good sense or logic fight their way back in where they were obviously not wanted or of any use.

Luckily, Timbers was on hand to lend a dose of reckless abandon to his thought process. "Sounds good to me. I mean, what else are we going to do? I say we do what the shelf says." With that, he sprang up onto the path upon which they had arrived, gesturing for his crew to follow.

Kate placed a hand on Marty's shoulder. "We'd better get going," she suggested, heading over to the pathway.

Marty squinted once more up towards the sunlit bookshelves and waved a hand in appreciative recognition. "Thanks for all your help."

"Don't mention it," came the whooshing reply from above as Marty joined Kate on the ascending pathway. "You would have done the same for me. Oh wait, you did do the same for me!"

Blustering laughter followed them as the group made their way back up the winding track which circled upwards into the sunlight. Pages whipped by them, caught in the chuckling breeze and flew in looping arcs down into the plunging depths of the paper fall, itself growing quieter and more obscure as they climbed. Even the laughter subsided while they trekked closer to the surface of the fissure. As they marched, Marty caught up with Timbers who was striding purposefully out in front.

"How do we find north once we get to the top do you think?" he asked, attempting to match the short pace of the miniature captain.

Timbers chuckled, retrieving a small brass compass from his coat pocket. "What kind of a ship's captain would I be if I didn't know how to use one of these?"

Marty nodded as they approached the surface of the fissure. "All right then, but how do we get to this station?"

Winking up at his companion, Timbers reached into his coat once more, producing a familiar looking tin whistle. "I refer your question to my first answer," he chirped with a twinkle in his one good eye. They arrived at the surface of the fissure just as the late afternoon sun set about bathing the paper torrent in its labored, deep orange glow. The river flowed like a huge, burnished bronze ribbon, emptying into the fissure behind them and twirling into the depths below, now dimmed by the retreating sun.

Hopping up onto a group of rocks, Timbers put the tin whistle to his lips and delivered three sharp blasts which cut into the fluttering silence like the protests of a model steam train. Vaulting up to join him, Oaf and Whipstaff sat and gazed up into the heavens.

Regarding the gradually sinking sun, Marty checked the watch that was not currently on his wrist.

Beside him, Kate gave voice to his concerns. "How long do you think it will take for them to get here? Assuming, of course, the Bobs managed to fix it."

As though in answer to her question, a sharp mechanical screech shot out of the sky and all heads craned in the direction it had sounded. Blotting out the waning afternoon sun as it approached, the Flying Fathom coasted silently towards the rocky outcrop. She was altogether more ramshackle than Marty remembered from earlier, but nevertheless, sailed towards them majestically through the low hanging clouds framing the sunset.

Atop his mighty perch, Zephyr angled his huge metallic wings, course correcting the galleon beneath him, and as they watched, he brought the Fathom to a hovering stop overhead. Heavy gusts of wind buffeted the group as Zephyr held the ship in place. From above, ropes dropped from the deck, coming to rest at just the right height for tiny cheering pirates and thankful people to clamber up.

The last to make the ascent, Marty hauled himself on deck to the sight of much backslapping and merriment. Standing proudly on the reconstructed deck were the Bobs, delivering and receiving high fives as they reunited with the rest of the crew.

"Look at her! She looks as good as new," Timbers crowed excitedly, hopping from one leg to the other and applauding. Marty surveyed the renovated Fathom. The deck had been nailed back together using additional wooden planks, and looked sturdy enough, but the masts appeared to have been fastened in place using palm branches and old rope. They creaked ominously as the great ship floated in the ether beneath Zephyr, but remained thankfully in place; for now, at least. All in all, she did not look at all as good as new, but she was airborne, which was all that mattered.

While Oaf and Whipstaff set about preparations to set sail, Timbers strode across the deck with the Bobs behind him. "And how's our old bird holding up?" he enquired, shielding his eyes from the setting sun and peering up at the avian automaton holding them aloft.

"Oh, Zeph is fine now," Bob chirped, nodding encouragingly.

"Yes, we just dumped him in the sea for an hour, quick oil change, and a couple of bags of bolts down his gullet; good as new," Also Bob continued, falling in alongside his twin and nodding in stereo.

Timbers turned towards his matching shipmates and grabbed each by the shoulder, beaming proudly. "Fine work, lads. Fine work!" He turned away just as quickly and trotted up to the bow of the ship. "Now get up to those nests, we set sail at once. North!" he called over his shoulder.

The Bobs complied instantly, and scurried up to their

respective perches either side of Zephyr.

As before, a complex chain of events was set into motion as Bob, Also Bob, and Zephyr performed their elaborate ballet of nod, sweep, and move, carrying the lurching vessel over to the right. Slowly the mighty bird steadied the Fathom, and more nodding and sweeping motions prompted him to lunge sharply forward, sending Marty and Kate teetering across the deck. With a shrill screech, Zephyr flung his wings in a downward arc, and the ship sped smoothly forward, much to the delight of Timbers, who oversaw the proceedings from the bow.

"And we're off!" he sang theatrically, swinging from the large mooring post beside him. "Next stop, Lucidity Junction."

The Fathom maintained a steady course, swooping and soaring through the sepia-tinged clouds through which the heavy evening sun filtered. They seemed to be making good progress, the land whipping by beneath them almost unnoticeable in the fading daylight.

With no immediate need to run, hide or leap recklessly from anything precarious, Marty ambled along the deck to where Timbers sat, gazing out at the horizon from his perch on the ship's bow. Sitting next to each other, hands on the rail of the deck, and eyes on the rolling hills up ahead, neither spoke a word as the minutes ticked by. Both knew this would normally be the time for platitudes, gratitude given, and quickly waved away because it was something the other would have done in their place. Neither had written a speech and neither had to, anyway, since they had known each other for far longer than just the one day when they had finally gotten around to talking.

Timbers glanced at Marty, seeming to sense what his companion was thinking, and chuckled. "Do you remember that time when you were six?" He giggled. "You came and dug me out of the garden after the neighbor's dog kidnapped me?"

Marty sniggered, nodding and smiling at the memory.

"And that time you were going to camp? You wouldn't get on the bus because your mum had forgotten to pack me?"

"I insisted we go back and get you," Marty chipped in, still laughing.

Now sporting a full on guffaw, the little pirate spoke again, "How about when you built me a pirate ship out of a cardboard box?"

"Yeah, it didn't last long in the garden pond though." Marty sputtered, laughing as hard as his pint sized cohort. Both continued to snort and chuckle for a few minutes, before the frivolity subsided, and Timbers turned to his friend.

Smiling, he extended a tiny cloth hand towards Marty. "I'm glad I got the chance to repay one of the ones I owed you."

It was a moment, and a sentence, Marty hadn't expected, and he hesitated before holding out his hand as well. The handshake was brief and slightly awkward, but didn't need to be anything else. It simply seemed the thing to do, even if it had not been needed to convey the feelings between them.

Timbers cleared his throat sharply, pulling them back into the moment at hand. "Come on now! Don't get all sentimental on me. We've still got a job to do."

As if to reinforce the point, a whistle rang out from the crow's nest above, and both peered up into the rigging. Bob was gesturing to a point just off the starboard bow and, as they turned to look, the ship banked in the same direction.

A cluster of lights punctuated the hillside, twinkling in the ever encroaching twilight. They ran in a group for a few hundred yards and then spaced out into a longer less illuminated line. As the Fathom drew closer, Marty could make out a huge glass dome, which appeared to be the source of the lights. Spanning out from either side, and lit by lanterns at intervals, was a large, looping track, although it appeared less like a railway and more like a rollercoaster. It pitched and dove sharply with rakishly angled turns and chicanes, which had no business belonging to a normal track.

The Fathom slowed, buffeting beneath the steadying wings of Zephyr, and gradually descended towards the dome. Marty rose to his feet and stared out at the almost ethereal structure before them. The dome itself radiated with a soft blue light that pulsed like a heartbeat. Although there was no shunting of trains or chattering of platform announcements, a steady hum seemed to allude to some sort of activity within.

Timbers scanned the ground beneath them with a

small brass telescope. "Well, there's nowhere to weigh anchor so we'll just have to hover outside." He shook his head disapprovingly. "Honestly, these places never have adequate parking facilities for airborne pirates."

Whistling up at Bob in his crow's nest, Timbers snapped his fingers twice before performing an elaborate hand gesture. Nodding, Bob turned to his doppelganger and relayed the instruction, which was in turn transmitted to the looming Zephyr. Observing the proceedings, Marty concluded that the gesture must have been an order to park, as the Fathom drifted gracefully into a holding position above the entrance to the dome. With a nod from his captain, Oaf pitched two rope ladders over the side, which toppled to the tarmacked car park a few meters beneath them.

With a second, smiling nod, this time towards Marty, the little captain swept a tiny cloth hand towards the edge of the deck. "After you, matey. You've got a train to catch."

Marty patted his companion on the shoulder warmly before vaulting overboard and onto the swinging ladder. This embarking and disembarking a flying pirate ship was getting worryingly familiar and, with a few short hops, Marty stood on terra firma, watching as Kate and the others descended from the Fathom. Further above them, Zephyr continued to hold the ship in places, flapping his mighty metal wings and sending gusts of wind surging down upon the disembarking crew. Within moments, they had reached the ground, and stood alongside Marty at the foot of a long flight of glass steps leading up to a pair of tall glass doors.

Timbers stood on the first step, calling over his shoulder as he hopped onto the second. "I'm going to stick my neck out and guess that this is the way in. Come on," he chirped as Marty gave chase. After twenty or thirty steps, and several protests that a place like this really should have an escalator, they arrived at the skyscraping entrance doors. Soaring to dizzying heights, they stood open invitingly, framed by a wide, colorful sign emblazoned with metallic lettering confirming that this was, in fact, *Lucidity Junction*.

The sun had started to join forces with the horizon behind them, and a deep orange glow sprang back from the letters, giving them an almost fluid look and further adding to the mysterious and transient appearance of the dome. Indeed, the whole surface of the structure seemed almost ablaze, dancing with reflected hues from the ebbing sun.

The group crossed the small courtyard and entered the dome, leaving the oranges and yellows behind, to be greeted by the blue iridescence that had been so prominent on their approach. The interior was stark, but no less impressive, boasting high reaching ceilings, flawless glass walkways, and seemingly endless rows of frosted glass seating. At regular intervals throughout the massive terminus, towering glass pillars emitted the pulsing blue light, which gave the interior its distinctive hue. As had been the case at Stellar Island, though, there was not a soul in sight.

"I bet they have a strict no stone throwing policy in here," Timbers chipped in as Marty scanned the vast chamber for signs of life. The pirate's little voice echoed ominously, drawing a nervous giggle from the little captain. This, too, echoed, although not nearly as ominously as the first utterance.

"Welcome to Lucidity Junction," A voice boomed from overhead, causing several sharp intakes of breath. Several eyes gazed in the direction of the voice, to a point at the far end of the hallway where a train itinerary was hung on the wall. Above it, a large public address speaker barked into life again. "Tickets are not available at this stop, since you already know where you are going, anyway."

Marty made a beeline for the itinerary even before the voice finished talking and traced a finger along the huge list of times and destinations as Kate and the crew of the Fathom caught up with him.

Peering up at the list, Timbers let out a short chuckle. "Will you look at that!" he cried, clearly amused at the list that stretched a good way up the wall. Each line seemed to give exactly the same information.

Time: When you get here – Destination: Everywhere

"Looks like we needn't have rushed as it doesn't look like you can miss your train." He giggled.

Marty turned to face them, a half smile on his lips. "No, it makes perfect sense. When you lucid dream, you know where you are and you can do what you like. When you get here, you just choose your destination and away you go."

Timbers' good eye widened. "Handy," he agreed, "Might be an idea to paint an X on the floor here and draw a map. This seems like a place I could get some use out of."

Marty nodded. "Why is it empty, though? It's like Stellar Island."

"No idea." Timbers shrugged. "Maybe you don't use this place much. As for Stellar Island, like I said before, who dreams of being at work? Why would anyone want to do that?"

Marty felt his face flush slightly, suddenly realizing why Stellar Island took up space in his dreamscape. He glanced over at Kate, whose similarly colored cheeks suggested she could hazard a wild guess. Diving headlong into a change of subject, Marty scooted over to the connecting doors that appeared to lead back outside.

"Look, there's only one platform," he said way too loudly. That made sense, too, he supposed. No need for multiple platforms when there was only one destination: Everywhere.

Moving outside and onto the platform, Timbers enquired as to the whereabouts of the train, just as a piercing horn signaled its approach. Again, all eyes turned towards the shrill intrusion as a shining silver, steam train pulled into the station. Although it appeared antiquated and out of place within such pristine surroundings, it seemed to be brand new.

The gleaming silver engine came to rest beside them, pulling behind it half a dozen immaculate chrome carriages. Steam poured from the engine's spotless chimney stack as it sat, almost purring, beside the platform. The doors to each carriage slid soundlessly open, offering a glimpse of the plush and lavish looking red velvet interior. All in all, it would not have looked out of place in a turn of the century murder mystery novel and yet here it was, sitting outside what looked like a cross between a futuristic spaceport and a giant inverted punch bowl.

Marty took a step towards the open doors of the first carriage, turning back to his friends just as he reached them. It had not felt like just one day in the company of these colorful misfits, and he found himself searching for the right words to say. A broad smile broke across Timbers' face as he spied the look on Marty's face. Trotting over to join him at the doors, the little captain offered up a hand to shake. Smiling, Marty grasped it firmly and attempted to formulate a goodbye of some kind.

"You know, I would never have made it here without your help," he began awkwardly. "I'd probably still be at home wondering why my reflection was talking to me."

Marty shifted his feet uncomfortably, still trying to verbalize his feelings in a way that would not have them both cringing. "I suppose I just wanted to say thank…"

"Come on now, we've been over this," Timbers cut in, giving Marty's hand a boisterous tug. "All I want to know is, did you have fun?"

Allowing a chuckle to burst the sentimental bubble that had begun to form, Marty nodded, fixing the tiny pirate with a look that passed on his thanks without the need for words. Looking past Timbers at the assembled crew of the Flying Fathom, Marty extended the same thanks. Gruff, manly nods were exchanged by all except Oaf, who's attention had been drawn away by a stray fluttering leaf, before Marty turned to Kate.

She stood beside him and peered in through the door of the first carriage. "Right, are we off then?" she enquired cheerily.

Before Marty could ask the question, she was already answering it. "Hey, I've come this far with you, it's not like I have anything better to do, and anyway, I want a go on this rollercoaster train, it looks wild." Beaming, she strolled past Marty into the carriage and took a seat. Looking from Kate, to Timbers, and back to Kate again, Marty realized if he'd stayed here for one day or a million days, he would never be too far away from surprise and bemusement. Raising a hand to wave one last time to his companions from the Flying Fathom, he turned and boarded the carriage, happy to be taking the last step of his journey in good company.

Another rasping whistle rang out and more steam billowed from the chimney stack as the train prepared to leave. The doors drifted shut, and Timbers called out to his friend.

"If you think on, have some piratey dreams. We'll go and look for treasure, eh?"

"It's a date," Marty replied, imparting another wave.

Timbers laughed heartily and shook his head. "Get going, ya big girl."

Almost in compliance to the command, the train shunted forward lazily, picking up speed and churning out more thick, white steam. Marty gazed out of the window, watching his friends grow ever more distant on the platform. Oaf had apparently noticed their departure and waved a hefty cloth paw as the train reached the end of the platform.

Marty took a seat by the window as the train picked up speed. They were soon heading up a steep incline that dropped away sharply ahead. He smiled. This did look like fun, and at the end of it, he would be back home with any luck. He glanced over at Kate, who was peering up the aisle between them.

"I think I'll go and see if there's a buffet carriage. We haven't eaten all day. Do you want anything?" she asked as she made her way through the deserted carriage. Smiling back at her, Marty shook his head and watched while she headed through the tiny door at the end of the aisle before turning his attention back to the window.

Outside, a familiar shaped appeared from behind the domed station, and veered in the direction of the departing train. Squinting into the fading evening sun, Marty opened the window and craned his head out for a better look. Soaring high above the train at a rapidly increasing rate of knots, the Flying Fathom pitched and turned so the tiny figures visible on deck could properly wave their friend off.

Marty extended a hand, waving back enthusiastically but froze almost immediately as a larger, darker shape appeared behind the Fathom. Dropping out of the twilight shadows, a huge airship drew alongside the markedly smaller pirate ship, blotting out the retreating evening sun. Almost entirely black, with jagged swathes of red striping its bloated frame, the enormous zeppelin drifted silently closer. On the deck below the dirigible, hunched figures lurked, their terrible grins visible even from a distance. As it passed over the Fathom, the figures leapt overboard. Marty's eyes widened as he realized what descended menacingly upon the flying pirate ship.

The clowns had found them.

They poured down onto the Flying Fathom like braying ghoulish hailstones. Something else had also landed heavily on the deck of the flying pirate ship, as it shook, shifted, and almost buckled with a splintering sound that Marty could hear from the train. As it pitched wildly to one side, barrels, boxes, and rope dropped overboard, forcing Marty to duck back inside the train as they plummeted past. He peered back at the Fathom as it was jolted a second time, sending more debris cascading from the deck.

Marty's eyes widened, and he recognized one of the

shapes tumbling towards him. It was Timbers shaped.

For the first time that day, Marty wished this had been one of the occasions when time slowed to a crawl. Staring wildly up at his falling comrade, he realized the seconds he had to react were annoyingly behaving like seconds, and were slipping by faster than he could process what was happening. Leaning out of the carriage, he made a desperate grab for one of the ropes that had fallen from the deck, now dangling beside the door from which he hung. Gaining a purchase on the rope, Marty glanced skyward just as the angry protests of the little captain came into earshot. Timbers was almost upon him, and Marty twisted sharply to face the descending buccaneer, holding out his free hand to catch him. Flashing back to games of catch he had taken part in as a child, Marty tried to ignore the fact that his sporting ability stretched to just watching as Timbers collided with him in a flurry of curses and pinwheeling arms. Luckily, pirates are a totally different shape to balls, and Marty managed to snag the little pirate's foot, halting his descent.

Timbers ceased his profane ranting and craned around to identify his savior. "Hell of a catch, matey!" he cheered. "Aren't you supposed to be on a train, though?"

Marty hauled his companion back in into the carriage. "I am. So are you, now."

Hopping back to his feet, Timbers was at the door in an instant, squinting up at the Fathom. "I've got to get back there. The lily livered bilge rats broadsided us!" he growled, leaping with surprising ease onto the trailing rope, and scurrying up it. Marty reached over as it swung back towards the train, and hoisted himself behind the climbing captain.

Timbers paused in his ascent and hollered back at Marty. "Where do you think you're going? You've got to stay on that train."

"I'm not going to leave you knee deep in clowns," Marty called out through the rushing wind. "We need to help the crew."

Timbers shook his head. "We can handle this. Get going. It'll be okay."

Dangling from the rope, Marty looked up at his tiny friend, and then back through the door of the speeding carriage next to them. He wished Kate would hurry up and get back from her search for sandwiches. He wished he had a plan. He wished he had a surface-to-clown bazooka.

Cursing, he swung himself back to the door, catching the frame and hauling himself inside. Above him, Timbers was climbing again, and higher still, the Fathom rocked erratically as Zephyr fought to maintain control.

The little captain reached the deck, hauling himself back on board just as more debris was flung past him and over the side. Much of this debris was clown-shaped, and was being ushered over the edge by a dervish-like Oaf. Spinning ferociously, he held out his mighty wooden mallet, catching everything that got close to him, and sending it toppling after the clowns he had already dispatched.

There were a number of the giggling interlopers still on deck, however, advancing menacingly with taloned hands outstretched. Behind them, Whipstaff vaulted masts and rigging as three more of the painted ghouls gave chase. From their crow's nests, the Bobs had taken to delivering death from above. Throwing anything they could get their hands on. Various objects crashed down around the hellish harlequins. One was felled by a coconut, another struck by a teapot, and a third was knocked to the ground as a toilet seat was cast heroically from the heavens.

Timbers surveyed the carnage proudly, not only because his crew were making short work of these scurvy dogs, but also because deep down, pirates just love carnage. He patted the cutlass at his side, a spare that he had fetched from his quarters, and strode purposefully into the fray.

The fight had largely left the remaining clowns, and they huddled together in a tight circle as the crew of the Fathom advanced, offering the simpering intruders only one course of action. Without hesitation, they took it, leaping over the side of the deck in a mass of shrieking, cackling, colorful chaos.

If ever there was a situation that called for a triumphant "Arrrr!" this was surely such an occasion, and Timbers delivered one of his finest.

"Was anyone keeping score?" he chuckled as the crew of the Fathom dished out slaps to the back and performed celebratory jigs.

"I think Oaf won that one, Captain!" Whipstaff piped up, aiming applause at his oversized shipmate.

Before the tiny giant had time to acknowledge the accolade, however, a huge, dirty white hand struck him heavily on the back, and he pitched forwards, skittering into the rigging across the deck.

The crew took a collective step back as a familiar throaty chuckle heralded the arrival of Mr. Peepers. Snaking out from behind the central mast, the towering, horrific figure of Peepers skulked out of the shadow of the sails and advanced on the crew. Shock at Peepers' sudden appearance sent them edging away from his advancing clutches.

Fighting clowns was one thing, but this was Mr. Peepers. To a man, they had heard tales while huddled around camp fires, and had seen the haunted looks on old sea dogs faces as they recounted them. He had been chasing them all day but now stood before them, bringing their worst fears into stark clarity. Peepers was almost upon them, and with no room left to retreat, the crew teetered on the edge of the deck.

Without warning, the hideous clown stopped and gave out an ear-splitting, bladder-squeezing wail, his bleach white face turned toward the sky as though howling at the freshly risen moon.

One of the Bobs stepped out from behind Mr. Peepers. Wide eyed and shaking, he pulled the point of a sword from the fleshy part of the baying monster's right buttock. Having stealthily shimmied down from their perches to aid their crewmates, the Bobs now stood in the firing line, as Peepers spun around to face his pint sized attackers. The demonic creature's eyes blazed with cold, insane fury, and his hand shot to his wounded posterior.

Sensing that some kind of captainly intervention was required, Timbers leapt forward, positioning himself between Peepers and the now cowering Bobs. "Listen here, chuckles," he spat, meeting the clown's gaze with one equally as intimidating. "You've got two choices. You can get back in your balloon and sail off over the rainbow or I can keelhaul you." The little buccaneer pondered for a moment before continuing. "Actually no, you've only got one choice," he announced, before hopping forward and kicking Mr. Peepers sharply in the shin. "Have at you, you big, googly-eyed git!"

Peepers sprang back, emitting a high pitched squeal of surprise and pain before sweeping a giant, gnarled claw at the fencing captain before him. Timbers caught the questing appendage with a wave of his cutlass, and it was withdrawn with another squeal. Clearly enraged but still chuckling, Peepers strode towards Timbers who danced back and forth, twirling his cutlass and shouting insults at his nightmarish foe.

The little captain ducked and weaved, swashed and buckled, before finally tripping on some stray rigging and falling on his face. In an instant, Peepers was on him, reaching down and plucking the pint-sized pirate from the floor and raising him to bulging, wild eye level.

Timbers twisted and flailed, trying to connect any sort of blow as Peepers raised him further in the air. Ceasing his chuckling, the horrific clown opened his mouth, wider than seemed physically possible, and wider still, like a grease-painted anaconda. Rows of jagged, yellow teeth drew back to reveal a thick darting tongue and a seemingly infinite black void behind them, as Timbers dangled helplessly above. Peepers licked his red painted lips and began to lower the wriggling pirate in his clutches into the gaping, tooth lined maw.

"Hey!" A voice sprang out across the deck, and Peepers jerked his head in the direction of this interruption.

Across the deck, Marty stood defiant, fixing his nemesis with an imposing stare he had seen countless times in movies. "Juggle this," he bellowed, pulling a rope attached to the cannon in front of him.

With a deafening boom, a cannonball launched towards Peepers, who held out both hands in an attempt to catch it. As he did so, Timbers fell from his grasp and dropped to the floor as the cannonball found its mark. Peepers let out a final, apocalyptic scream that seemed to drown out the thunderclap of the cannon.

Marty wiped soot and dust from his face as the smoke cleared. On the deck where Peepers had stood, a single oversized shoe lay on its side, smoke issuing from the empty space where a foot had been moments ago.

Next to it, Timbers sat upright and turned to Marty.

"Did you just fire a cannon at me?" he grumbled, trying with limited success to suppress a smirk. "And 'Juggle this' was my line," he protested, the smirk melting away into a full blown grin.

Marty shrugged. "What can I say? I couldn't very well beat the bad guy without saying something clever, could I?"

Punching the air, Timbers ran towards Marty, apparently realizing after a few steps that his crew was watching and a hug wouldn't be very piratey. Composing himself, he doffed his hat towards Marty and stood aside as the crew of the Fathom raced over to offer their congratulations.

Amidst the cheering, whistling and applause, Timbers made his way over to the edge of the deck. Peering down over the side, he glanced back towards Marty. "Are you forgetting something, matey?" He pointed downwards as he asked.

"The train!" Marty cried, his eyes widening.

The Bobs were already scaling their masts as Timbers raised a calming hand.

"No need to get in a flap, lad, we can make it." The hand performed a complex gesture, which was relayed to Zephyr by the Bobs, and in an instant, the Fathom was plunging towards the rapidly departing train. In another instant, they were almost alongside as the carriage weaved and dipped on the manic track. As Marty pondered how to get back on board, Oaf and Whipstaff hefted a large wooden beam from where it had been secured to the central mast. A half smile spread across his lips as he realized what the beam was for, a realization confirmed when it was laid flat and pushed out from the edge of the deck, creating a makeshift walkway from the Fathom to the train.

"This is the best part of being a pirate," Timbers cheered, motioning for Marty forward. "Walk the plank, me hearty!"

Marty began to laugh along with his pirate comrades, when a glance over the side saw his nerves interject. It was a long way down, and the plank only extended halfway. Not only that, but the train was twisting along the track so wildly that the Fathom was struggling to stay alongside. Edging along the plank, Marty summoned all the courage the day had shown he had. The train straightened, but the relief was short lived as Marty shot a glance to his side. A few hundred feet ahead, the track plunged into a tunnel that radiated with fierce white light. Those few hundred feet were being eaten up rapidly as the train and the Fathom sped onwards, and suddenly the battle between Marty's fears and his courage were forced to take a backseat.

It was now or it was never, and realizing this, Marty took one last look over his shoulder.

Timbers beamed his toothy, mischievous, smile at his friend one final time. "See you soon," he called as Marty leapt across the ether between the Fathom and the train.

Sailing through the air, the thought that Marty may

not have gauged the jump correctly took hold as the doorway fell away in front of him.

Grasping hands that fell short of their target met with something else, however. Marty looked up, and into the eyes of Kate. Gripping his hand tightly, she hauled him into the carriage just as the car ahead of them entered the tunnel.

The Flying Fathom veered away sharply, and Marty heard the defiant and triumphant screech of Zephyr as the carriage was bathed in brilliant light and everything turned white.

Light poured in through the bedroom window as Marty opened his eyes with a start. For a moment, he felt blind as his eyes grew accustomed to the intrusion of the morning sunshine. Gradually though, the familiarity of his bedroom fell into blurry, then sharp focus.

Marty sat bolt upright in bed. He still felt the roaring wind that tugged at him only moments earlier. His hand still gripped tight, as though holding onto something, someone. His mind still raced, and the faint whiff of soot and gunpowder hung in the air.

Getting out of bed, he hurried across the room to the wardrobe. Pulling the door open, he scanned the interior. Shirts, coats, shoes, and general junk sat in the quiet darkness, acting exactly how you would expect shirts, coats, shoes, and general junk to act.

Closing the door, Marty headed out into the hallway.

There, the large wall mirror stood unbroken, casting his reflection in perfect detail. Peering closer, Marty's image copied him identically. Marty made a face, the mirror image replied in kind. A smile was met with a smile. A stuck out tongue was copied. There seemed to be no disparity between Marty and his reflection.

Hurrying back into his bedroom and pulling the curtains fully open, Marty gazed out at the world. It was raining, and the postman was making his way up the path. In the street, a bus chugged past, all four wheels firmly on the floor and an actual driver at the helm. The sound of letters hitting the mat recaptured Marty's attention, and he made his way out of the bedroom to inspect them. Sifting through the bills and circulars, he made a stab at ordering his thoughts. If he was still in the dream, he really needed to have a word with himself if all he could manage were bills and circulars. If he wasn't still in the dream, what exactly had happened over the last twenty-four hours?

A ringing in his ears snapped him back to reality. It was the phone, and Marty raced once more into his bedroom just as the ringing stopped. Picking up the phone, he pressed the blinking answerphone button.

"Hi, Marty. It's Kate…from work. Listen, I had the strangest dream about you last night. I was thinking we should talk. If you want to." There was a pause during which Marty could almost hear the blushing on the other side of the phone. "You have my number. Give me a call."

Sitting on the bed, Marty felt a smile break across his

face that would not soon be moved.

Punching numbers into his phone, and buoyed with the confidence gained from a day spent in his own head, Marty cleared his throat and waited for the dial tone.

He had one hell of a dream date to organize.

About the Author

Arriving in the rainy isle of Great Britain in the late '70s, James quickly became an enthusiast of all things askew. Whilst growing up in a quaint little one horse town that was one horse short, a steady diet of movies, '50s sci-fi and fantasy fiction finally convinced him to up sticks and move to Narnia - also known to the layman as Wales. Since there was no available qualification in talking lion taming or ice sculpture, he settled for a much more humdrum degree in something vague but practical, and set out to find a talking lion to make an ice sculpture of.

Mystifyingly finding himself behind the desk of a nine-to-five job, he kept himself sane by singing in a rock band, memorizing every John Carpenter movie ever made, and learning the ancient art of voodoo. Finally deciding to put his hyperactive imagination to good use, he ditched the voodoo and picked up a pen. A few months later, his debut novel, The Forty First Wink, was born. With a clutch of short stories in the offing, James is now loving his new life as an author, and still sings when plied with alcohol or compliments.

He also recently developed a penchant for fiercely embellishing his past. He really was a singer, although The Forty First Wink may not have brought about world peace. *Yet*.

Thanks for your purchase!
Please post a review on
Amazon or Goodreads (or both!).

Also stay tuned for book two of
The Forty First Wink series,
The Fathom Flies Again, coming from Ragnarok
and James Walley in 2016.